A HEART'S WAGER

Eva Copperfield has lived a life of poverty in the squalid slums of New York — until a sudden inheritance gives her the chance of a new life as lady of the manor in the English countryside. Her journey from rags to riches is complicated by the mysterious Ben — who is either a lord or a charlatan! Eva has to navigate the Atlantic and her heart before she can find a home . . . and love. Wagers are being made. Who will win?

Books by Heidi Sullivan
in the Linford Romance Library:

GIFT OF THE NILE

HEIDI SULLIVAN

A HEART'S WAGER

Complete and Unabridged

LINFORD
Leicester

First published in Great Britain in 2008

BROMLEY
PUBLIC
LIBRARIES

AL

CLASS
LPB/F

ACC
03059214

UL   INVOICE DATE
1 8 DEC 2017

First Linford Edition
published 2018

Copyright © 2008 by Heidi Sullivan
All rights reserved

A catalogue record for this book is available
from the British Library.

ISBN 978–1–4448–3546–5

Published by
F. A. Thorpe (Publishing)
Anstey, Leicestershire

Set by Words & Graphics Ltd.
Anstey, Leicestershire
Printed and bound in Great Britain by
T. J. International Ltd., Padstow, Cornwall

This book is printed on acid-free paper

Bromley Libraries

3 0128 03059214 4

SPECIAL MESSAGE TO READERS

THE ULVERSCROFT FOUNDATION
(registered UK charity number 264873)
was established in 1972 to provide funds for
research, diagnosis and treatment of eye diseases.
Examples of major projects funded by
the Ulverscroft Foundation are:-

- The Children's Eye Unit at Moorfields Eye Hospital, London
- The Ulverscroft Children's Eye Unit at Great Ormond Street Hospital for Sick Children
- Funding research into eye diseases and treatment at the Department of Ophthalmology, University of Leicester
- The Ulverscroft Vision Research Group, Institute of Child Health
- Twin operating theatres at the Western Ophthalmic Hospital, London
- The Chair of Ophthalmology at the Royal Australian College of Ophthalmologists

You can help further the work of the Foundation
by making a donation or leaving a legacy.
Every contribution is gratefully received. If you
would like to help support the Foundation or
require further information, please contact:

THE ULVERSCROFT FOUNDATION
The Green, Bradgate Road, Anstey
Leicester LE7 7FU, England
Tel: (0116) 236 4325

website: www.foundation.ulverscroft.com

1

Strands of titian hair escaped from beneath Eva Copperfield's old wide-brimmed straw hat as she gazed up in awe at the *Baltic*, one of White Star's finest liners. The sun's blaze hit the whiteness of the ship, sending the rays dazzlingly back out into the New York harbour. People shielded their eyes with hands or newspapers as they looked up at the impressive structure that was to take them to Southampton, England.

The vast harbour was filled with all manner of passengers milling about, from the first-class travellers barking orders at valets and maids to those travelling steerage third-class calling to excited children who ran alongside the *Baltic*, chattering to each other in many different tongues.

It was April 1910. The Golden Age. Eva wondered just who thought it was so gilded; certainly not anyone she knew. Perhaps England would be better. Maybe then she'd know how Golden life could be.

Eva was to join the third-class passengers. Her meagre belongings fit into one large burlap bag; her clothes were of rough worsted and cheap wool. She looked down at the itchy brown skirt and the worn boots that were a size too big because they were her late father's and she had been unable to afford new ones. The jacket she wore had thinned with use, the fabric on the buttons now rubbing off, the cuffs frayed. *Soon*, thought Eva, *I will be able to buy all the jackets and dainty boots I want.*

Unlacing the bag for what seemed like the thousandth time, she peered inside and smiled to herself. It was still there, nestled amongst the small bundles of underwear and the one dress she owned — a dress of white cotton trimmed with lilac ribbon that had been a birthday gift from her parents before

. . . Eva stopped this train of thought abruptly. *Eva Copperfield*, she scolded herself firmly, *there is no use dwelling on the past. Your mother and father are no longer here; you must follow the path you set out on.* And the package of papers in her bag was the beginning of that journey.

'They're boarding!' an excited voice, deep with a Russian accent, cut through her reverie. The first-class passengers moved onto the ship, their clothes the height of fashion, their maids and valets struggling beneath cases and hat boxes.

Those due for steerage watched them. Eva suspected that there were many eyes filled with envy. The taverns and bars pressed together around the dock were now emptying. Men rushed out to see if they could earn a dime or two helping those with hand luggage, as some were hauling their bags and boxes out of the public houses towards the dockside with no valet to assist them.

Eva's attention was caught by a trio of men who stood arguing amiably in loud, strident voices. Two were obviously from the upper echelons of society; their polished shoes, pristinely pressed suits and ebony walking canes attested to that. The third man, however, could in no way be termed 'quality'. Dressed in a thin greying shirt, oilskin waistcoat and moleskin trousers, with a brown and green flat cap atop his ash-brown hair, he was indeed tall and handsome, though still obviously not a social equal to the other men with whom he was bantering.

'I can't believe you're going through with this,' the shorter of the rich men, his hair gleamingly macassared, said to the poorer man. 'It's ludicrous!'

'And *your* idea,' said the man in the cap cheerfully. 'So here we are. I shall do it, you'll see!'

The third man, plump and whiskered, laughed. 'Well I'll say this for the blackguard — he don't miss a trick!' This man had the quick, lively manner of an American, his accent placing him locally from New York. The other two men were both English.

Suddenly, Eva realised that the poverty-stricken man was looking at her, a frown creasing his smooth brow. No wonder the man was staring at her with a quizzical expression: *she* was staring at *him*! Feeling the heat rise to her cheeks, Eva lowered her gaze, embarrassed at being caught eavesdropping.

'Well, I'll be boarding now, sirs.' The man who had had his eyes turned to Eva bowed theatrically, causing his small companion to snort with derision. 'And I will carry off this plan, you see if I don't. The money's mine, gentlemen, and don't forget it!'

Their eyes had not met again, and Eva saw him slip into the knots of steerage passengers now waiting to board. She clutched her bag closer to her side, her thin cotton gloves bunching as she gripped it. She could not afford for it to be taken by the pickpockets she knew must be moving around amongst the passengers. The papers Eva Copperfield carried were too precious to be out of her sight.

Still feeling ashamed at having been found to be listening to the conversation between the men, Eva waited until she could be sure that the tall fair-haired man had found a place in the boarding queue. She took a few moments to retrieve her boarding pass, which she had secured with a pin to the inside of her bag. After carefully unpinning the white slip, she read it again: *White Star Line — Third Class Number 1871888*. This thin square of white paper would be her ticket to a new life.

Eva made her way to join the queue, clutching the pass in her gloved hand, noticing as she did so that her nail had worn a ragged hole in the tip of the thumb. In two weeks she would be in England. In two weeks she would be claiming her inheritance. She would own Fern Lodge.

★   ★   ★

Upon boarding the *Baltic*, the third-class passengers were given a very quick examination by the team of surgeons situated at the head of the gangway. Eva had noticed that the higher-class travellers had not had to be seen by the foxy red-haired doctor. They had simply boarded and no doubt been greeted with smiles and charm.

Those heading for steerage were poked briefly, eyes checked as a precaution against any signs of illness, and hustled along to the stewards. More than a dozen were turned away.

When Eva's turn came, she found that she was shaking. Her fingers clutched her bag, her throat suddenly terribly dry. She certainly felt well enough, and could not imagine that this doctor would see any problem. He looked down her throat, lifted her eyelids, and took her pulse. With a nod, he waved Eva on. She was able to board. The shaking in her limbs began to slow and her heartrate calmed.

'Single men, this way please!' The

steward to whom she had been directed was a young-looking man with a high brow and a look of cheerful resignation to his post. 'Women and children to the left. Down the stairs and along the corridor. The steward there will guide you further.'

A press of women threatened to carry Eva off her feet. She allowed a few who were herding small children to pass, then she too began the descent into the deep hull of the boat, which was to be her home for the next two weeks. Once there, she took in her surroundings: plain whitewashed walls with very little else to relieve the monotony. She wondered what decoration adorned the walls of the first-class apartments.

Beyond the stairs, the knot of people that Eva had managed to get tangled up in had landed at the start of a labyrinth of passages and corridors. A steward with the same look, same uniform, same nondescript-ness about him stood patiently as women and children gathered in small clumps, the many tongues rising in a cacophony worthy of Babel's tower.

After a few moments, he held up his hand. 'Ladies! I shall take your tickets, record the numbers, and then direct you to the bunks as necessary.'

Of course there were those who did not understand English, so the clamour began again, with the women obviously concerned about what was happening. Eventually, after much fuss and exasperation, the steward managed to safely deploy the correct passengers to the correct quarters.

Eva found herself in a small, square room with two metal beds and two carved wooden chests. There was little room for anything else, but it was newly painted; and when she put her rough bag of paltry belongings on the bed, a thread of scent — of freshly-laundered linen — rose up into the cabin.

She was debating with herself whether to simply choose this bed or wait for the other passenger who would share these quarters, when the door opened and in walked a pretty and pleasantly plump girl, her hair the blue-black of a raven's wing, her eyes startlingly clear blue.

'Hello there!' she greeted, her accent an Irish brogue that placed her to the south of the Emerald Isle; she had the soft lilting vowels of the country, not the harshness of the city or the north.

'Hello.' Eva watched as the newcomer threw herself onto the bed opposite the one that held her own bag.

'My, and isn't this a fine room?' She smiled up at Eva. 'You won't mind if I take my boots off? My feet are as sore as a bareback rider's bum.'

Stifling a smile at this girl's free way of speech, Eva began to unpack her bag. As she did so, her new roommate sat wiggling her toes, obviously relieved that they were free from the pinching footwear than now lay discarded in a heap by the bed. Eva was putting her few items of clothes into the chest when she noticed a cardboard tag affixed to the Irish girl's battered case. *Niamh Kelly*.

'You say my name like this — 'Neeve',' the dark-haired girl said, now rubbing her stockinged toes.

Eva blushed a little at being caught reading the label, even though it was, of course, there to be seen by anyone. The warmth in her cheeks cooled, however, when she saw Niamh smile.

'So now you know my name, what's yours?' Niamh wriggled her feet one final time and sat forward, resting her arms on her knees as though ready to listen to Eva and any tale she might tell. 'I love a good yarn, so tell me, what are yer doin' here?'

Eva had finished folding her belongings and had placed them in the chest. All that remained in the burlap bag was the sheaf of documents. She would sleep with the bag under her pillow. Niamh was nothing if not patient, and she sat watching Eva, who stood up, rubbing the ache that had begun in the small of her back.

'My name is Eva. Eva Copperfield,' she said, now sinking gratefully onto the bed facing her new friend.

'Eva.' Niamh nodded, as if approving of the name.

'I used to live in Manhattan with my parents, until . . . '

The screech and creak of the carriage as it swung out of control, and the squeal of the horses as they fled, panicking at the weight they were pulling behind them when all they wanted to do was run untethered . . . The little clean but sparse cabin and the plump colleen were gone, replaced by the bitter memory of being orphaned. Eva had lost everything: her parents, her home, her comfortable wealth. Until now . . .

'I am an orphan,' she continued. 'My parents were killed when dogs scared the horse pulling their carriage. We lived quite comfortably, but soon I realised how little money they had left. The house was repossessed and I had to move to quarters in the Lower East

Side. I took a job in a coffee shop.'

All this time her companion had listened, the blue eyes never wavering from watching as Eva twisted the heavy material of her skirt in her small hands, or closed her eyes briefly as the memories towered, threatening to engulf her. Niamh never spoke a word, yet her very presence was louder and more comforting than any banal niceties she could have said.

'And so,' Eva continued, after a deep breath, 'I decided to do something. I decided that one option was to move to England, to London — see if the streets really are paved with gold.'

Niamh sat up a little straighter, her cheap corset creaking as it strained against her fleshy figure. 'Sure, an' I'm not one to pry, an' I don't want to push yer, but . . . I don't think yer tellin' me the whole story, now are yer?'

The truth of that statement, so plainly put, and yet said without an ounce of malice or pique, threatened to send Eva into tears. Niamh had, in the space of the short time she'd known Eva, seen the tightness with which she carried herself.

A lump had lodged painfully in Eva's throat, and she swallowed against it. She gave Niamh a smile, knowing without needing a looking-glass that it was weak and watery. She could feel it stretch her lips, but it did not warm her eyes. Niamh gently patted Eva's hand as it lay trembling on her lap.

'I'm sure it'll work out, pet,' she said gently. 'Whatever's troubling you, it'll be fine once you reach England.'

But that was just it. Eva's problems would only start when she was in England. For when she finally arrived in Sussex, she would need all her wit and resolve. She would arrive at Fern Lodge as the daughter of Granville Copperfield, trying to claim her inheritance, plucking it out of the hands of her Uncle Jonas. The uncle who did not even know of her existence.

2

Eva wasn't surprised that Niamh had so quickly ingratiated herself. She was warm and charming, a natural at setting people at their ease. Eva, however, knew she was too unsure of herself, too dazed still by the events of the past few weeks. She had kept to the cabin, unable to meet with people socially until she felt that she could find her feet. Niamh had brought Eva food from the dining room and had tried, to no avail, to coax her new friend from her self-imposed seclusion.

'You must get out of this room sometime,' protested Niamh, her hair now gleaming. She turned to Eva, the brush waving admonishment as she spoke. 'Eva, pet, whatever is botherin' yer, it might be made more bearable by talking tattle with folks. Give an' get the blarney, that's what I say.'

'You go on, Niamh,' Eva answered. 'I'm tired and do feel quite queasy. Seasickness I suppose.'

Niamh shrugged. 'Please yerself, but I intend to dance tonight. I think Joe — you remember I told you about him from the dining room yesterday? Well, he invited me. Maybe I'll dance a jig with him.' Her large eyes glittered, and the soft, full mouth became a wide smile. 'Reckon he could be sweet on me!'

Smiling back, Eva said, 'Then enjoy your jig.'

After pulling her ample frame into a frilly blouse of dove grey and a cheap but handsomely cut skirt of blue broadcloth, Niamh twisted her dark hair into a knot, securing it with pins and two jaunty red ribbons. One last inspection in the looking-glass brought a satisfied smile to her face, and with that, Niamh Kelly left the cabin.

Now that she was alone, Eva lay back on the bed. The mattress was surprisingly comfortable, the sheets of excellent quality. In fact, she had heard that on some White Star liners the quality of the steerage was almost that of some of the older liners' first class. It was certainly better than the vermin-infested rooms she'd had to rent since the death of her parents.

After the carriage accident, Eva had endured the bitter cold of their December funeral. The ground had been frozen, almost too hard to dig. She had stood by the gaping blackness of the grave, watching the coffins as they were lowered together to be encased forever in the cloying black earth. Her hands had numbed from cold and she'd had trouble throwing the clod of earth onto the coffins. The thump on the wood of the coffins was the loudest sound she'd ever heard. When it was over and the plumed horses had moved off, their breath feathers of mist rising from their flaring nostrils, Eva Copperfield was left to ponder her future.

She sat up now from the bed, the memories too harsh and still too sharp.

The *Baltic*'s motion was not so very much, just a rocking, a swaying that told her that the sea was calm. Hugging her knees to her chest, Eva allowed the ship's list and roll to soothe the bruises her soul had suffered.

After the funeral, there had been the realisation that there was not much money. The house had been repossessed, the bailiffs had removed anything of value long before that, and Eva had been left with a shell. She could find nothing in her parents' paperwork to indicate that there was a will or any assets. She presumed that they had died intestate and that her fate was to be an orphan of no means.

It had been March when all that changed. Eva had found a small damp room overlooking the Hudson River. The river mist and the dankness found their way into the very fabric of the building. The tenements were noisy with children, shrill women, giggling and cat-calling girls and stray dogs, yapping and snarling in the yard as they foraged for scraps and caught huge rats.

It was into this melee that Mr Jude Upton had come, his nose screwed up against the smell, his small weak eyes squinting behind gold-rimmed spectacles as he made his way towards Eva's room.

Eva had seen him from her window. He had been walking along the road that ran parallel with the river, looking up at the buildings and consulting a piece of paper. And when the landlord knocked on her door, his piggy eyes obviously seeing money somewhere in all this, Eva was shocked to see that the man she'd been watching was standing right there.

'Miss Copperfield?' His thin hand actually trembled as he held it out to be shaken. Poor nervous man, having to leave a warm office to visit this rat hole.

She was too surprised to be embarrassed by the mould on her walls or the filth on the rugs. She ushered him in, shutting the door on the landlord and his greedy mind.

And thus Eva Copperfield was informed that she did indeed have an inheritance. When her father had gone to America, he had left the estate of Fern Lodge in his brother's hands until such a time as he returned or until a child of his inherited. Jonas, as the second brother, would inherit only if Granville died childless or intestate.

There was a will, and there was a child — Eva. And the will had stipulated quite plainly that even a girl would inherit all. And so, with a loan arranged by the kind and eminently practical Mr Upton, she was able to pay a month's rent and book passage to England. She chose steerage so as to keep some money behind.

'Your uncle is, as far as I can ascertain, unaware of your existence,' Upton had said as Eva looked over the various papers, deeds and documents with him. 'It seems there was some animosity between him and your late father.'

So her Uncle Jonas would have a

shock when he saw her. But she had long since decided that she would be fair. She would not simply wrestle the estate from him. She would discuss terms, living arrangements, and so forth. After all, it had been his home. But Eva owned the land, and knew that no man would take kindly to having to do business with a mere female, niece or not.

The ship suddenly swayed a little, then calmed again as if sighing. Eva wondered if Niamh had had her jig with Joe yet. She also found herself wondering about the mysterious passenger whose eyes had met hers on the dockside. It occurred to her that she had not been close enough to see what colour they were.

She shook herself, stretching out cramped limbs. What a ridiculous notion! What did his eye colour matter? But somehow she felt that it did. Snatches of the conversation she had overheard between the three men now snagged in her memory. It had all sounded decidedly odd. The steerage passenger in particular had intrigued her. What had he been doing, talking to such rich men? What money was his? Had what she'd heard been the discussion of a crime that was going to be committed? There were so many wealthy travellers on the ship that a crook could have rich pickings.

Niamh had been badgering her to go to the party in the General Room ever since she'd heard about it. Well, in for a penny in for a pound. She would go. She needed to meet with people, talk, and slough off the despondency and melancholy.

The white and lilac dress was the only decent thing that Eva had to wear. She shook out the material and held it up to her slender frame. The dress was cut close to the figure, the décolletage high, trimmed with a muslin collar.

After dressing quickly, she looked upon her reflection in the tall mirror on the wall opposite her bed. The dress skimmed the ground, its patterns and fastenings ornamental, with scrolls of embroidery and tiny lilac buttons, a small lace flounce finishing off the three-quarter-length sleeves. Eva's hair hung loose, red-gold in the light from the cabin's lamps. Twisting and curling it into a few hairpins, she managed to fashion it into a softer style.

But she was still pale. It was as if the death of her parents had bleached her of colour, the grief and subsequent hardship sapping the robust and healthy complexion and turning it into a thin, pallid ghost of what it had been. She pinched her cheeks and nibbled at her lips. A little colour returned, and Eva felt that she could finally show herself in public.

* * *

The General Room was a pleasant surprise. Larger than Eva had anticipated, it was tastefully decorated with pine panelling and white paintwork. Someone was happily sitting at a piano banging out a merry Celtic tune, a few pint glasses already sitting empty on the top of it. The piano player was being accompanied in his endeavour by a few equally merry musicians. They played accordions, tin whistles, and someone was even rattling a pair of spoons against his knee. And there in the corner of the room, now cap-less, with his ash-brown hair falling a little too long around his ears, stood the man she'd been musing over.

Eva felt her knees weaken. She had, of course, expected him to be here, but seeing him was an altogether different matter. He held a half-pint pot, and was leaning against the wall, talking and laughing with a smaller man with dark whiskers and ape-like features.

Suddenly Eva's elbow was tugged. She was startled and froze.

'Eva, pet! How wonderful that yer joined the shindig!' Niamh hugged Eva warmly and plucked at the flounce of her sleeve. 'You must come and meet Joe.'

Niamh led her towards the piano, where a group of men stood singing a song that seemed to bemoan just about everything and anything. Despite the depressing words, the song was being sung with aplomb and enthusiasm. Eva wondered at the optimism these people had and wished that she shared it.

Joe was a man of medium height and build; his hair a mousy brown, trimmed to an acceptable length; his eyes a warm brown, like milky tea. But when Eva saw Niamh's own sky-blue eyes light up upon seeing him, she knew that he was far from mediocre to her mind.

To be fair, when Joe spoke he showed a quiet intelligence and manner that could not help warming anyone to him. He was from Hell's Kitchen, a squalid and fearsome part of New York to which many Irish immigrants had migrated. Niamh shuddered and shook her dark head as he described his life there.

'I'm going home to Cork,' Joe said finally. 'Me father has a farm. I'll stop

25

in England for a few months and rake in the money a bit, labouring or some such. Then when I've made a bit o' brass, enough to bring home to him, I'll go an' help him and me brothers.'

'I'll go home to Limerick one day,' said Niamh, a dreamy cast to her full features. 'But first I'll away to London and seek my fortune, so I will. I'll work as a maid, an' move up to lady's maid. Then, when I've made me money, I'll be off to my little home by the Shannon, so I will.'

Eva knew what was coming next. Joe and Niamh looked at her, expectation written on both faces.

'And you, Eva,' Joe said softly, 'what'll be your plans?'

She sighed heavily. 'I plan to find my uncle in Sussex,' was all she said.

'You lucky thing,' Niamh said. 'To have family waitin' for yer.'

'He doesn't know that I'm coming.' Eva suddenly felt self-conscious. Niamh and Joe had turned their full attention on her, and she did not want to talk.

'Oh, what a grand surprise for him.' Joe had finished the pewter mug of porter and had placed the cup on one of the polished tables scattered around the room. 'Ah, it's our song, Niamh.'

Niamh giggled. 'Now, Joe Barrett. We don't have a song, sure we don't.'

'We do now!' Joe took Niamh's hand and they tripped off to the little square of floor that had been cleared of tables, benches and chairs to create a make-shift dance floor. Eva watched them whirl and spin, a look of pure happiness clear on both of them.

'Would you care to dance?' The voice came so suddenly from behind her that she almost leapt from her skin, her heart beating a painful tattoo beneath her ribs.

Her stranger!

'I have been hoping to see you ever since we spied each other at the docks.'

She could not tell if her cheeks had blanched or warmed their colour. In her attempt to speak, all she could manage was a stutter. 'I . . . '

'Pleased to meet you at last.' A large hand was held out to Eva. In turn she offered her own small fine-boned fingers, and found them swamped by a hand that was warm and as soft as a puppy. 'My name is Ben, by the way.'

'Eva.' She was immediately on her guard. Ben gave the impression of being a man whose only work could be physical — the hard graft of a dock worker, oil worker or ranch-hand. And yet his hands showed no sign of having ever held hoe or shovel — no calluses or blisters, no rough hardened skin. Why, then, was he dressed in such poor apparel?

'Well, Eva, will you dance?' He was certainly English — his accent betrayed him as such — but Eva could not have placed where. She knew nothing about England.

'Yes.' Dancing with this man would give her a chance to learn more about him.

By the time they had negotiated the little clusters of people to reach the square of dance floor, the tune was a slower, more melodious one. It was haunting, played beautifully on the panpipes by a wrinkled walnut of a man with a shock of white hair and a full snowy white beard.

Ben was a good head taller than Eva, and he smiled down. 'Perhaps this is a waltz?'

'I . . . don't know how to waltz.' She was aware of the hands taking her own, an arm round her waist. The dance floor was now depleted. It seemed that only couples were dancing now. Prickles of cold sweat began beneath the linen of her gown.

Despite her protests at not being able to dance, Ben had Eva in a waltz-hold and they were moving around the other dancers with an ease that surprised her. His feet were perfectly placed not to tread on her toes, and a hand rested just so in the small of her back so as not to seem too familiar.

Despite the formality of his stance, and the fact that they were in a room full of many other people, it felt to Eva as if they were in the midst of something private and deeply personal. Her eyes were everywhere except Ben's face; she had never known a dance to last so long.

As they glided, with Eva inexpertly picking up the steps, she began to feel the knots of tension in her shoulders and limbs loosen. She eventually looked up at Ben. His aquiline nose and high cheekbones rested well together. In fact, the more she took in the features — the Cupid's bow of his lip, the small creases at the corners of his mouth as he smiled — the more she would have said that he was handsome.

At the end of the dance, the tight muscles bunched in Eva's neck had relaxed, and she had become quite proficient at the waltz. Ben bowed and took her hand. He brought it to his mouth and gave it the merest brush of his warm lips. Eva quivered.

'Thank you, Eva,' said Ben.

Eva saw now that his eyes were a

green-blue, the blue of calm pools with sunlight glinting off them. But despite all this, there was one nagging thought in her mind. This man was not what he pretended to be. Wherever else he should be, it was not steerage. Soft hands, an ability to dance a waltz with perfected ease, and the manner of one far above the class he maintained he belonged to all told Eva that this man was lying.

3

The party ended with the steerage passengers drifting off to the different berths segregating men and women. Niamh and Joe stood together, pressed into the corner of the room, Niamh's dark head close to Joe's mousy one, talking in earnest.

Eva watched the two and saw a closeness building, a bond that she had never really known with anyone. She looked surreptitiously at Ben, who was sitting next to her; a sidewise, sliding glance that she hoped he'd not seen. He was finishing his ale, swallowing down the dregs in the bottom of the glass, and did not appear to have noticed Eva's eyes upon him. She cleared her throat in order to speak and politely take her leave, when he turned full upon her and said, 'I'd like a walk out on the promenade. It's really rather stuffy in here. I should welcome some fresh sea air.'

Eva, too, had been thinking how hot the room had become. The smell of beer, bodies and cigarette smoke was beginning to make her dizzy. The brisk saltiness of the Atlantic would clear her head of both the odd thoughts she was prone to and the mugginess that had filled it like cotton wool.

Ben was retrieving his jacket from the back of a chair. 'Eva? Shall we?'

Heart fluttering, Eva smiled. 'Yes. I'm ready. The fresh air would sure be a change from this room.'

The north Atlantic in April, Eva soon realised, was beset by ice. As they walked out of the room onto the promenade, a cold blast bit into their faces and gloveless hands. Eva had not brought any wrap and had only the thin threadbare jacket with the faded elbows and shabby buttons. The gloves she had were not much warmer than having bare hands.

No doubt seeing her shiver, Ben took

off his jacket and placed it around Eva's shoulders. Her muscles became rigid at the shock of his touch. Despite the fact that they had been dancing in each other's arms for what seemed like hours, this simple act, this innocent touch of fingertips on her shoulder, sent such shivers down her tingling spine that she feared she might fall over.

'Thank you,' Eva said. 'But I don't want you to get cold.'

Ben shrugged; an elegant lift of broad shoulders. 'I'm fine. I like the cold. I feel too warm for the jacket anyway.'

Hands folded together to keep them warm, Eva watched the sea speed past the boat's rails. The water was like tar now in the night's darkness. The *Baltic* slid along, passing the jagged black shapes of icebergs and a sprinkle of light in the distance that Eva took to be another ship. The cloudless sky was patterned with pinprick stars: tiny perfect diamonds threaded onto black velvet.

'Are you all right, Eva?' Ben asked,

now stopping, his hands clutching the rail as he looked out to sea. 'I fear it is rather bitter now.'

'You do need your coat,' she said with a smile. 'I appreciate your gallantry, but there's no use getting a chill. Let's go inside.'

He grinned back. 'Well, maybe I'm not as hot-blooded as I thought. Still, let's just walk to the end and use the stairwell there. It will, I believe, lead us back to steerage.'

Despite the strange beauty of the sea's vastness in the night, it was really becoming too cold to stay. But Eva did not want to end this. She pulled the coat around herself and nodded. 'So long as you don't freeze over. I doubt I'd know what to say to a snowman!'

Ben laughed. 'The walk will warm me up. Besides, I have more meat on my bones than you.'

Eva took a sharp intake of breath and threw Ben a look that she knew must shout her hurt. His personal comment had not been meant unkindly, but it had struck her heart with the accuracy of an arrow. Yes, she was thin. Yes, she was pale and undernourished. She felt little more than a mouse now, whereas just moments before she had been verging on being a princess.

'I didn't mean to offend,' Ben said hastily. 'I just . . . ' His voice faltered. 'I apologise.'

Eva gave a brittle smile. 'Don't worry. Come on, let's go inside.'

Their walk continued, both now absorbed in their own thoughts. Eva wondered what Ben was thinking. His face was puckered and creased, as if a worry or concern had settled on his brow and wasn't going to leave until contemplated and mulled over. Eva's own thoughts were a muddle.

The remark he'd made had been throwaway. It had been a simple observation, but had hit a raw nerve. She was jittery about how she was going to manage the transition from pauper to landed wealth. Ben had reminded her in a flash of searing light just who she was, and would probably always be: a simple nobody from Nowhere, New York. Thinking that she could manage her inheritance was foolish. How could she?

Since her parents' death, she had not managed to cling to anything. All material possessions had been sold or used to pay off debts. She knew not a dime's worth about land or estates. She was just a skinny mouse, with only her pride and a bag of papers.

Somewhere, a band was playing Gilbert and Sullivan. An operetta, Eva thought. She had seen some of their musicals with her parents, enjoying them as special treats. Snatches of *The Mikado* caught on a fresh gust of wind, and she could almost see a bright theatre, its gas lamps lighting up the gilt on red velveteen chairs, the stage a rainbow of colours and costumes. And her parents smiling indulgently at their only daughter as she sat enraptured by it all.

'Are you all right, Eva?' Ben took her

elbow. 'I have upset you. I'm so sorry. It was unforgivably clumsy of me to make such a rude comment. It was simply that I thought you needed the coat more than I did. I don't think I'm a very good Sir Knight. Instead of saving a damsel from distress, I have made a damsel distressed.'

'You must understand what it's like,' Eva answered, not laughing at his lame joke, even out of politeness. 'I mean, you are travelling steerage as well.' She stopped walking and looked up into the handsome face with its aquiline nose and high cheekbones. Once again, and for the thousandth time, she was struck with the conviction that Ben did not belong among the tatters and rags of steerage. 'You, too, have no money.'

He took a breath and looked away briefly, as if he'd heard a noise behind him. When he turned back, his face had lost any sense of concern or worry. There was no attempt either at jollity or bad jokes. His features had settled into a serious expression.

'Eva, I don't know what you have been through. But I know what *I* have been through, and what I have seen people suffer. I don't belittle you or patronise you. Never think that of me.'

This bemused her. He seemed to see this as an answer, but it answered nothing. It just clouded and evaded what she had been trying to find out. Eva still did not know him, even though she had opened the way for him to tell her his story. He must be hiding something, she told herself.

'Ben, I think we really should be going in now.' She took the coat and gave it back to him. 'The stairway is there.'

He nodded and silently put on his jacket. When they reached the iron stairs leading back to the third-class quarters, Ben took her frozen hand and brought it to his lips. 'Eva, please don't be cross with me. I am a private man, and sometimes my thoughts run along tracks I don't wish people to follow.'

Feeling stiff with cold and misery,

Eva could only nod dumbly as he turned to leave. She watched his broad back turn the spirals of the stairs and disappear into the belly of the ship. She followed slowly after a while, smelling the pungency of the steerage quarters, strong and foul after the bracing open air.

When she returned to her little cabin, she found that Niamh was already asleep. Her breaths came deep and even; a settled slumber. Her ebony hair was splashed across the white of the pillow and the covers were pulled up to almost touch her chin. A small smile played on her full lips, and Eva envied the trouble-free dreams she was obviously having.

After washing and slipping into her thin cotton nightdress, Eva finally slid under the covers of her own bed and closed her eyes. But sleep would not come.

In her sleep Niamh sighed and, now loose-limbed and relaxed, turned in the bed. The springs complained a little and the cover moved, but she did not wake. Eva longed for Niamh to do so. She wanted to tell her of her time with Ben; to discuss, dissect, rearrange and examine every moment of the walk on the promenade. She needed Niamh's wise words. But Niamh slept on, her breathing now little contented snores.

★ ★ ★

The journey was nearing its end. In less than two days, the *Baltic* would dock at Southampton and Eva would have to leave to make her way in a strange country. She and Niamh had become close friends. Indeed, Niamh was Eva's only friend. It was hard to allow her mind to accept that they would soon be going their separate ways. Eva would be truly alone.

She often walked along the promenade, feeling more and more jittery about what awaited her in England. Now, just before lunch was due to be served, Eva was watching the water flow past in flurries of white-capped froth. Gripping the rail, she allowed the wind to blow salty spray into her face.

'Are you all right, Eva?'

The voice startled her from her reverie. It was Ben. His smile sent tingles through her. She steadied herself and smiled back. 'Ben! I've not seen you for a while. Are you well?'

He grimaced. 'A touch of seasickness, I'm afraid. I'm not a sailor.'

Eva was full of sympathy; the journey had not been altogether smooth at times.

'But,' continued Ben, 'I feel much better now. Ready, I think, for some light lunch.'

'So am I.'

'By the way, I think you need this.' He handed her a handkerchief.

Eva frowned in incomprehension.

'Your face — it's wet from the sea spray.'

'Yes, I suppose it is.' She thanked him and dried her face.

His nearness was pleasantly distracting, and she was at a loss for words. A couple walked by, chatting and gazing adoringly at each other. A honeymoon couple, Eva suspected. A child raced past chasing a hoop. Eva watched and then turned back to Ben.

'We are nearly in England. What will you do when you are there?'

Ben looked out over the water. The breeze played with wisps of his hair. Eva felt that he was on the verge of telling her something important. After a silent moment, he took a breath.

'Eva, I . . . '

Then the gong sounded, calling passengers to their meal. Ben looked as if he could have easily cursed, and Eva felt a stab of disappointment. What had he been about to say?

Ben offered her his arm, and she slipped her hand into its crook. 'I must say that I am becoming quite excited about seeing England again,' he said as they made their way to the dining room.

'I take it that England is home, then.'

He smiled. 'Yes. I have been in

America on . . . business. Now, I am ready to go back to London. But I'm bored already with talking about me. Let us talk about you.'

'There is nothing to talk about. I have left America to go to my uncle in Sussex.' Eva tried to sound as if this was of no great importance, but she could hear the tremble in her voice.

'Ah, how exciting! And your family in New York — they have allowed you to travel unaccompanied?'

Eva looked down at her too-large boots. 'My parents were killed in a carriage accident. I have no family in America anymore.'

'Oh, forgive me!' Ben stopped and looked at her, his face full of anguish. 'Here I go again, saying the wrong thing to you.'

'Please don't worry. You didn't know.'

'But you have family in England, you say? Good, good. Then you will be cared for.' He nodded as if to himself. 'That's good.'

They had arrived at the dining hall.

Eva pushed open the door and was hit by the smell of food and the noise of steerage passengers enjoying the fact that this was one place they were not segregated. Men sat by wives they saw only at meals or in the General Room. Fathers sat with their children on their laps. Newly minted love affairs blossomed all the stronger as sweethearts sat close. Eva found a bench with space and pointed it out to Ben. 'We can sit over there.'

'You don't mind sitting with me?' Ben's eyes twinkled with mirth. 'I mean, I seem to be putting my foot in my mouth at every given opportunity!'

Eva managed to grin at him, warmed by his concern for her. 'Just put your food in your mouth, not your feet, and we will be fine!'

'Good advice.' Ben pulled out the chair for her, then sat beside her.

Eva suddenly felt ravenous. Her spirits lifted, and she found herself enchanted by Ben's humour and the easy manner with which he spoke to the people on their bench. *Could this be the start of something?* she mused dreamily. *Because I am certainly falling for this man.*

* * *

Eva was making her way to breakfast on the day of the docking. She was full of anticipation, and her heart fluttered every time she thought of Ben. Now well used to the labyrinthine twists and turns of the steerage quarters, she was not really thinking about the way she was heading, and it was only when she heard male voices that she realised she had taken a wrong turn and ended up in men's steerage.

She was flustered a little, trying to get her bearings. She hoped no one would see her; what would they think? She was just about to turn back when she heard Ben's voice.

'I have done it. Surely you can't deny me the money?'

Eva stopped, frozen. She recognised

the next voice that spoke as that of the plump well-dressed man she had seen talking to Ben at the docks in New York.

'The ship has not docked yet. We want you safely off before we give you a dime.'

'Can I trust you?' Ben was saying.

'Yes! Just wait until she docks, get off the boat, and I shall write your cheque. Then you and your women can be as happy as pigs in muck. I confess to being surprised that you have pulled it off. No one suspected?'

Eva felt sick as Ben laughed. 'No one! I did it without anyone suspecting a thing. I shall await your cheque. My ladies will be glad of it.'

'And the kiddies too, eh?'

'Ah, the children. Yes. Your money will help keep my women and children warm. I am sure they thank you.'

Feeling dizzy and faint, Eva dashed back up the stairs and found her way back to her cabin. Women and children? No one suspecting? Ben was nothing but a charlatan. Eva flung herself on her bed, glad that Niamh was at breakfast.

Hot tears stained her cheeks. Ben was lost to her. He had been of a criminal bent, and she had allowed him into her affections. Well, no more. He was banished from her thoughts. She was not going to be another of his 'women'.

* * *

The *Baltic* arrived at her destination on time and with a flourish of whistles and clanking metal. Eva was on the deck, watching the dock come into view, opening out before her with its warehouses and myriad moored vessels. The ship pulled into a slender stretch of water, swinging past a smaller tugboat that hooted petulantly at the near miss. The channel widened out a little, the *Baltic* slid alongside another White Star liner, and the process of securing her safely began.

Southampton on that morning was

warm, with a fresh breeze and clouds the colour of dusty lambs scudding across a watery blue sky. The air was heavy with the sharp, fishy tang of the sea, and gulls whistled and screamed overhead. The dock was full of people. Eva held back and stood beside Niamh, watching the to-ing and fro-ing.

Ben had been nowhere to be seen since she had overheard that dreadful conversation. Now, with disembarkation only minutes away, it looked as if she had lost him forever. And good riddance, she thought bitterly. She need never see him again.

The gangway was lowered, and an excited thrill ran like so much electricity through the passengers. As people pressed to make their way down the gangway, Eva stood on the tips of her toes, trying to crane her neck over the heads of the pushing, pulsing mass of people. But Ben was not there. She would be able to make it without bumping into him.

The tide of steerage passengers

swept Eva and Niamh off the boat to land on the dockside, bags in hand and looking around in bewilderment. They had decided that they would both go to London. Eva needed to speak to the solicitor whose name she had obtained from Mr Upton. Niamh had been given the address of an order of nuns from a priest at St Patrick's back in New York. She hoped to lodge at their refuge on Crispin Street until she found work. The father knew a priest who was on the committee for the refuge and whose position on that committee was to find work for the girls who stayed there. Father O'Toole had been sure that Niamh would quickly find employment, as she was bright and a 'good girl'. Niamh's rosebud of a mouth had twitched when she related this to Eva.

'That father never did hear my confession. T'was always Father Moriarty there on Fridays!' she said.

But Eva knew full well that she'd be hard-pressed to find someone with a

50

bigger heart than Niamh Kelly. They would both lodge there, and the next morning Eva would make her way to Sussex and her unknown destiny.

They boarded the train to Waterloo from a specially built platform on White Star's ocean dock. After settling into the blue broadcloth seats, they waited for the train to pull away. Niamh soon fell asleep, leaving Eva to watch as they passed moors and downs, the train pulsing and rocking through chalk tunnels or rattling past thatched-roofed cottages and fields of purple heather, the landscape dotted with trees that she could never have named.

Coming as she did from the slums alongside the Hudson River, with its rats and warehouses and reek of rancid water, Eva was captivated by the English countryside. The green freshness and the sheer expanse of it enthralled her. As the train stopped at stations with names she tried to remember — Eastleigh, Winchester, Woking — it struck her that soon she'd own land like this. Maybe Fern Lodge would resemble the proud isolated manors sitting firm on the brows of hills or tucked into the valleys. She began to build a faint picture of what the house might be like.

Soon, however, the half-timbered and stone quaintness began to fall away, replaced by brick houses with slate roofs that stood in dismal rows blackened by smoke and smut. The smoggy atmosphere came from the mills and factories that loomed over the houses like spiders over flies. Warrens of tenements and slums, punctuated by the iron roof of a factory every so often, sped past the train window. Soon they would be arriving in London.

It was not long before the train pulled into Waterloo. Jogging Niamh's elbow to wake her, Eva peered out at the station: a Victorian mishmash of a place topped with a steel and glass roof.

Niamh woke, her blue eyes widening as she realised that the train had stopped. 'Is this it? Is this London?'

'Yes,' Eva said, gathering up her bag and pulling on her frayed jacket. 'This is London.'

4

Providence Night Refuge and Convent stood a little off Crispin Street on land that had once been set aside for fairs. The rooms were solidly built but sparse. The Sisters of Mercy who ran the shelter assigned Niamh and Eva a room and told them to report to Monsignor Chapman after evening prayers.

It was decided that Niamh would go and change the few dollars she had while Eva went to find Mr Hanbury, her father's English solicitor. As she did not know her way around the great capital city, she decided to spend a few pence on a growler. The solicitor was easily located in the Inner Temple. Unlike Mr Upton, Victor Hanbury was a jolly, corpulent man who laughed much, even when the joke was not immediately obvious. Money had been released for Eva, the papers checked.

Hanbury shook her hand. 'Well, Miss Copperfield, you are now a lady of means. The rents from the cottages on the land, plus a percentage of the sales from Lodge Farm produce, are enough to keep you comfortably. And there are at least thirty acres of land that you could quite easily sell, for they are not really doing anything.'

Eva's head was a whirl. She could not begin to think about selling land, or rents or farms; this was all so new to her. Simply signing the few papers that she needed to, she took the brown envelope back from the solicitor and thanked him.

She decided not to take a cab back, as she wanted to see London — and more importantly, clear her head. She'd be making her way to Sussex tomorrow and would have to meet her unknown uncle and any family he might possess. Eva considered this as she found herself on Blackfriars Bridge.

All rivers smelt and looked the same,

she thought. The ugly swirl of the Thames was much the same as the Hudson. Murky and unformed, her reflection showed a thin, peaky girl, not a woman with her own wealth. Her hair was escaping from its pins and ribbon, and her eyes were large in her pale face. The money now in her handbag weighed heavily; never had she possessed so much. Clutching the bag close, Eva began to worry about thieves and pickpockets. Perhaps she should be making her way back to the refuge. After one last glance at the water, she moved off the bridge to locate a cab.

★   ★   ★

'And I picked up *The Lady*, and a paper.' Niamh scrutinised a pile of clothing that she had emptied out of her carpetbag. The two friends were back at the refuge and had taken up their room.

'There is a job for an under-parlourmaid at a big house on Conduit

Street,' Niamh said. 'I walked past, and sure if it wasn't the grandest place you ever saw.' She wrinkled her nose at a moth-eaten and tatty fur wrap. It was ginger, and Eva could not tell what animal it had once been. 'I'll have to get rid of this.' Niamh threw the wrap on the floor. 'How did you get on, pet?'

Eva had not told her the whole story, so Niamh did not know that Eva owned Fern Lodge. All Eva had mentioned was that she was going to the solicitor to receive money kept in trust for her until her father died. 'I got my money.'

Turning from the pile of clothes, Niamh smiled. 'Oh, that's grand. You'll have no worries getting a train to your uncle's place then.'

Getting a train would not be a difficulty. Eva's problems would begin when she arrived and declared to an unsuspecting family that she now owned their home and land. A deep gut feeling had prevented her from writing to Uncle Jonas. She wanted to tell him face to face what needed to be said.

'Are you going to apply for that Conduit Street job?' she asked Niamh, wishing to steer the conversation away from her uncle.

A tawny-brown blouse dropped to the floor. 'That's not my colour, and 'tis ripped here. Pardon? Oh, yes. I don't see why I shouldn't have just as much chance as anyone else.'

'True.' The blouse looked to be of good quality, and Eva wondered why Niamh was throwing it away. It wasn't as if she had money to spare to buy new clothes.

Eva surreptitiously surveyed the pile. It was a ragbag of odds and ends — a red skirt, a blue jacket, and even a pair of green men's trousers. 'Niamh,' she ventured, 'where did all these clothes come from?

'Oh, a charity. There's a Mission Hall in Stepney; I went and pleaded my case. I got all these — free. 'Tis all the fine stuff the rich ladies don't want.' She held up a beautiful black taffeta skirt. It was a few years out of date from what Eva had seen being worn by the fashionable ladies of London, but with knowledge of needle and thread it could be turned into something lovely.

Niamh's brow furrowed. 'Now that'd never fit me, even if I didn't eat for a week. How skinny was the wench who squeezed her poor little body into this?' She smoothed her hand over her own ample rump and stomach. 'No, this is like a babby's size on me.' She looked at Eva, and a smile began to form. 'But on you . . . ' She held the skirt up against Eva and pursed her full lips. 'Mm, if you just took it in here and pulled this here . . . '

'I can manage with sewing,' Eva said eagerly. 'I'll mend the blouse too, if you like.'

'Oh, you have it if you want. It won't suit me. Come here and we'll sort this lot out together. Pick what you want.'

By the time they had rummaged through the clothes, Eva had, amongst other things, the brown blouse and a good pair of boots that fit as if made for her. They were of kidskin, and of such soft creamy texture and colour that she couldn't understand how they had stayed in such good condition. But then, the grand London lady who had worn these was hardly going to trudge around in mud and grime. She'd have a carriage.

Eva twisted her feet around, looking at the boots from every angle, feeling how perfect they were and realising that she now had the means to be able to keep them clean.

★ ★ ★

The journey to Fern Lodge had been too swift, in that it did not give Eva enough time to gather her thoughts. She had taken the train from London to Crawley, and from there found a train bound for the village of Fernthorne. Fernthorne station was tiny — one solitary platform and a dilapidated station house. The stationmaster sat in his cupboard-like office and looked as bored as anyone would be in such an out-of-the-way place.

'Excuse me.' Eva tapped on the glass of the office door.

In his surprise, the poor man slopped his tea over his regulation blue trousers and, frowning, came to the door. He slid back the glass and peered out. 'Yes, miss?'

'I need to get to Fern Lodge. I'm afraid that I have no idea how to get there.'

He scratched his head. 'Jonas Copperfield's place? T'aint a long walk. I reckon you could do it in maybe twenty, thirty minutes. Else you could try and catch a trap or cart as is going that way.'

The idea of walking was not unpleasant. Eva didn't mind stretching her legs and making the most of the wonderfully green openness.

'I could walk. If you'll be so kind as to tell me which way.'

'You'll need the road that leads from here, miss.' He pointed down a country

61

lane that wound back behind the station. 'It leads up through the village. Then you'll need to find your way through the country lanes. The Lodge is back a bit. It's a bit of a twisting route, I'm afraid, but not too bad. Pass the church and carry on. You'll come to Hobston Lane. Walk up that till you see a white gate with a gravel drive. Sign'll say 'Fern Lodge'. That's yer place.'

'Thank you. I'll try that way then. Goodbye.' Glad of the new boots, Eva began to walk. The village had a single winding street, at the north end of which lay a green.

Eva could never, in all her imaginings, have created something so oddly quaint as this tiny village. Georgian buildings hemmed in the green, their sash windows and cast-iron railings painted glossy blacks and bottle greens. As Eva made her way up the street, a trap pulled by a dozy horse with feathery fetlocks and dusty flanks passed by.

The May sun, though still quite

watery, made a gallant effort to warm the place. The walk was enjoyable, and became even more so when Eva reached the dappled, shady lanes. Serenaded by birdsong, she wound her way along chalky white paths and tracks of dried mud until she came to the start of a long, sweeping driveway.

The sign, painted with faded black paint on a now-dirty white board, proclaimed 'Fern Lodge'. The drive curved around a clump of trees, but as Eva peeped between leafy branches, she could just make out three chimneys. With her stomach in knots, she made her way along the drive, feeling the crunch of tiny stones beneath her feet. How would she be received here? She walked up the curling drive until there before her lay the house.

Built of honey-coloured stone and standing amongst beautifully mani-cured lawns edged by woodland, Fern Lodge was not as intimidating as Eva had expected. In fact, the house was much smaller than she had imagined.

Its mullioned windows were like benevolent eyes rather than the fearsome orbs of an ogre. Ivy wound its way up the walls, making the whole building informal and inviting. As she stood staring at the place, she had to remind herself that she now owned it.

A perky little maid with bright eyes and a frizz of dark curls let Eva in and led her to a study off the main entrance hall, where she bade her to wait. It was only a few moments until the door opened and a man walked in, a questioning frown drawing his brows together.

'I am Jonas Copperfield. You wished to speak to me?' he said.

Uncle Jonas was the sort of character that Charles Dickens would have been proud to have created. Almost painfully thin, he stood a little over six feet tall. With eyes large behind thick spectacles perched on a beak of a nose, and odd tufts of snowy hair, Uncle Jonas resembled nothing less than an emaciated owl.

Eva cleared her throat and pulled her shoulders straighter. She calmly explained the situation. Apart from a flicker of eyes and a bobbing of his Adam's apple, Jonas showed no real reaction to Eva's story. When she had finished, he simply peered at her, his expression unreadable.

'So you are my brother's child?'

'Yes, I am.' Eva clutched the strap of her bag as Jonas rose from the creaking leather chair.

'They passed away in a carriage accident, you say?'

'Yes, sir. A carriage accident.'

Jonas blinked twice. 'My poor brother and Emily. He married well. My sister-in-law, your mother, was a very decent woman.'

Eva was sure that she could trace no real sadness in her uncle's voice. She doubted that the news of her parents' death had pierced the emotions of this man. That was, if he had any emotions.

Just as Eva was about to add more to her story, the door to the study opened, and in glided an elegant woman. Her blonde hair was bound up in ribbons of ice-blue velvet that matched her dress. Both her figure and face were waspish, despite their beauty. Sharp grey eyes sat large in a perfect peach of a face. Her mouth, although full and soft, was drawn into a disapproving line. If her demeanour hadn't been so cold, she could have been a fairy from a child's book. Following her were three fawn and brown lap dogs that growled softly and cowered behind her skirts, glaring malevolently.

'Ah, Kathryn, my dear,' Jonas said, his voice strained and tight. 'See who has come to visit. Only the daughter of my dear brother. Tragic news, Kathryn. Granville and Emily have . . . they are lost to us in an awful accident.'

The insincerity of the man stung Eva. His wife raised arched eyebrows and said, 'Indeed? How . . . sad. And they have left you penniless by the looks of it.'

Eva pulled her shoulders back and

opened her mouth to speak, but Jonas jumped in. 'We will talk to Eva tomorrow. She is tired from her journey and will need sustenance and rest.'

'But Jonas, if your brother has left us a waif, how are we to feed it?'

'I will cause you no undue concern,' Eva said coolly. 'In fact, I think you should know that I have been left Fern Lodge and its estates by my father. I will, of course, discuss this with you. I assure you that I will not give you any difficulties.'

Kathryn's face blanched. 'You own this house?' she shrieked. 'Jonas! How can this be true?'

At her shrill voice, one of the dogs leapt up from where it had been sitting by its mistress's feet. It yapped and flung its tiny body around the room, followed by the other two dogs, which yelped and growled at nothing in particular.

Kathryn clapped her hands together. 'Shh!' She sat on a large leather chair and held out her arms to the dogs. All three animals, trembling and panting with the sudden flurry of excitement, rushed towards her. They hurled themselves onto her lap, nipping and snapping at each other in order to win the best place on her full skirts.

'Calm yourself, dearest.' Jonas rolled his eyes. 'Go to your room and rest. Our niece is quite right; she will not give us any cause for alarm.'

The words chilled Eva. The unanimated expression of her uncle did not fool her. There was something darker behind those thick spectacle lenses.

Turning to Eva, Jonas spoke calmly. 'I will get one of the maids to show you a room. Please take a seat and I will find someone to help you. Then, you will of course want to eat in your room. I will arrange that.'

Kathryn shot Eva a look filled with vitriol and swept off, velvet skirts whispering and hissing as they brushed the carpet. Jonas left too, his hands twisted together, and with not so much as a glance back at Eva. After a brief moment, a sullen maid came to take Eva to a room.

After trudging up the stairs to a room located on the third floor, the maid passed through a door with its white paint peeling and showing splitting woods, and its crystal door-knob very worn and chipped. This door led to a dark and dismal corridor lit only by puddles of amber light thrown by old gas lamps. The rest of the house had been connected to electricity, but this wing was obviously neglected.

'Mr Copperfield says to stay here for tonight. Then he'll have a proper room done up for you in the morning.' The maid took a key from the voluminous pocket of her apron. She unlocked the door and, with a kick of her booted foot, it opened.

Eva stepped in behind her. The room held two beds and a dresser. A wardrobe was pushed into an alcove on the far side.

'I'll fetch you something to eat, Miss

Copperfield.' The maid bobbed a churlish curtsey and shut the door behind her.

The view from the window made up for any amount of odd uncles, spiky aunts and truculent maids. It even compensated for the sparse, characterless room. A lake glittered in the sun, and the perfectly laid lawns were carpets of emerald velvet. Beyond the garden were woodlands and open fields. The panorama opened out like a painting. It was perfect. Eva threw open the window and was greeted by sweet air. A rap on the door meant that she had to turn reluctantly away.

'Come in,' she called.

It was not the maid who entered, but a girl of about Eva's age; her hair the same chestnut, her eyes the same hazel. The girl rushed forward and took both of Eva's hands in her own. 'How wonderful!' she enthused. 'Harriet, the maid, told me all about you. She's a terror for listening at keyholes, that one, but she came running to tell me that you are my cousin!'

Eva nodded, momentarily bewildered by this vibrant intruder into the room. The girl slapped a hand to her mouth and gasped. 'How rude! I haven't introduced myself. I'm Dora, Jonas and Kathryn's daughter.'

A cousin. Eva allowed her hands to be squeezed in Dora's warm clutch.

'We'll be great friends,' Dora continued. 'It's so nice to have someone here of my own age. It can be terribly dull. Oh, I have friends, of course; but Mother can be a bit stuffy, you know. I suppose since you're family, she won't be so difficult.'

Dora prattled on. Eva listened. After a few minutes of Dora describing her life at Fern Lodge, she finally paused for breath. Grinning, she said, 'I expect you're fed up with my natter. I shall leave you to settle in. This is an awful room, isn't it? But Father will no doubt have one of the guest rooms made up. You'll have to forgive being pushed in here for tonight.'

'It's fine, really.' Eva tried unsuccessfully to stifle a yawn. 'I am really sorry, but I'm tired. I'll just freshen up and eat, and then I'll be able to see around the place.'

Dora nodded her agreement. 'I shall hurry up your lunch. I think Father said you'll be eating in here.'

'Yes; I need to look through my things and sort them out. I may even take a nap, if that's all right.'

'Fine.' Dora gave Eva a hug. 'It's so nice to have you around. After you've sorted yourself, I'll give you the guided tour.'

5

The light lunch and hot, sweet tea revived Eva. After a quick freshen-up, she tentatively made her way downstairs. She found Dora in a library off the main entrance hall. Her cousin had curled herself up on a large plush chair and was engrossed in a doorstep of a book. Intent on the thick volume, Dora did not notice her cousin's arrival; but after Eva had hovered uncomfortably around for a minute or so, she looked up, startled.

'Eva! Have you rested? You look better. Shall I show you around?'

'I don't want to disturb your reading. If I may, I'll look around the place myself.'

The book snapped shut, the page marked by a thin rectangle of silk embroidered with an intricate design of oriental origin. 'I'd not dream of it. I'd love to show you around, Eva. It'll be a pleasure.'

The cousins made their way out of the front door and on to the gravel of the drive. Turning west, they wandered towards the lake and the beautiful lawns that Eva had admired from her window.

'The sunset here is truly wonderful,' Dora was saying. 'It seems to set the lake on fire.'

Eva followed as Dora made her way to a bridge that crossed over a small stream flowing from the lake. 'Where does this stream go?'

'To a water wheel, but no one actually remembers what the wheel was supposed to work,' Dora answered. 'We think there was a mill, but it must have been destroyed. Now, if we cross over here we come to the gardens.'

The girls wandered through carefully tended rose gardens and vegetable patches. Eva felt the tight muscles in her back relax as the warm sun filtered through and the fresh air cleared her city-clogged lungs. Eventually Dora led her back to the house, entering now through a side door and heading up a flight of incredibly narrow stairs.

'I like these stairs. No one uses them, not even the servants. They lead to a small landing; you saw the part of the house jutting out on the wall overlooking the stream? Yes? Well that is a bit added to the house by my grandfather. No one has told me why, but I've been in there and noticed a bedroom and a sitting room, like a lady's room. I reckon he had a fancy woman!' Dora pushed open a door at the top of the stairs, and Eva saw that this led on to a dark square of landing with rooms coming off three sides to it.

'I used to play up here and hide when I was little. No one ever found me, you know. I think it's been forgotten.'

Eva followed as Dora pushed open a door. They entered a sitting room with shabby furniture. The carpet had been re-cut from another room — the pattern of green splashes that Eva took

75

to be leaves was too large for the room.

'It's so Victorian,' Dora said. 'You'd not think we were in 1910, would you? But I've never been disturbed up here; no one ever comes here anymore.'

Dora led Eva through to a bedroom, even smaller than the sitting room. Flinging herself onto the brass bed, Dora said 'It was so exciting, the first time I found this. Everything was covered in Holland fabric. It felt so strange to pull off all those dust covers and discover all this.'

'Do you still come up here?' Eva asked.

'Oh yes. Not as much as I did when I was little, but yes, I still do. Usually to get away from my mother.' She smiled wryly. 'Oh well, I think we ought to be getting back. You must be exhausted.'

Eva had to admit that yes, she was tired. She gratefully followed Dora back out of the tiny rooms and back to her own bedroom to rest.

The bed was uncomfortable — as hard as the ground. Eva kept waking up to odd sounds that she told herself were just the creaks and sighs of an old house. Eventually she managed to fall into an exhausted sleep.

★ ★ ★

The light of the morning bled through the slats of the blinds, waking Eva. Tired and groggy, she lay until she had allowed the day to seep into her.

She swung her legs out of bed and padded over to the window to open the blinds. She looked over to the lake and saw Dora sitting on a bench, reading. Eva was suddenly struck with the desire to go wandering in the gardens and catch a breath of fresh country air.

Cold water had been left in the chipped porcelain bowl on the dressing table, and Eva shivered as she washed with it. Pulling on a blouse and skirt and the new kidskin boots, she looked at her reflection in the time-speckled mirror. After arranging the folds in her skirt and pulling her hair up into pins,

77

she went to open the door.

She pulled and pushed at the handle, shaking the door as she did so, but the door was stuck fast. This part of the house was old and nowhere near as well-maintained as the rest of the lodge — she remembered the maid having to kick at it when she'd first arrived. Maybe the door was stuck because the wood had swollen.

Eva tapped on the glass of the window. At first fingertip-soft taps, then knock-bruising panicked bangs that threatened to dislodge the glass from its shaking frame.

Eventually Dora looked up and frowned at the house.

'Dora!' Eva had no idea if her cousin could hear her. She pulled open the window. 'The door's stuck!'

Lifting up her dove-grey skirts, Dora tripped up the stone steps towards the house. She stood beneath the window, shielding her eyes and squinting up to Eva.

'Are you all right, Eva?'

'The door's stuck.'

Signalling that she was coming up, Dora disappeared from view. Eva sat back down on her bed to wait, feeling foolish. But it was not her fault that she had been placed in an old neglected wing of the house.

There came a knock on the door and a rattle of the brass doorknob.

'Can you open it from out there?' Eva called.

'No.' Dora's voice came muffled through the thick wood. 'I'll have to get the maid. I expect she'll have a trick to opening it.'

'Thank you.' Eva sighed and went back to look out of the window. Aunt Kathryn was strolling across the lawn, the three fawn and brown terriers scampering at her heels. Eva knocked on the window, but even though her aunt glanced round to see where the sound had come from, she did not seem to see her.

When Eva's pocket watch showed that she'd been waiting nearly twenty minutes for either her cousin or a maid to return, she began to worry. Where were they?

In fact, no one returned. By dinner-time Eva was alternating between frantically shaking the door and banging on the window until the glass rattled in the frame. By dusk she had given up and sat, disconcerted, on the bed. What had happened?

The next day she tried calling again through the door. This time, it was not long before she heard the tapping of boot heels on the uncarpeted landing and a key grating in the lock. Relief washed over her like welcome rain after a draught. The same sullen maid entered, carrying a tray. The smell of a large, steaming-hot breakfast of bacon, toast and eggs made Eva's stomach growl with hungry anticipation. She had eaten only lightly the day before, and no one had brought her food since.

'The door was stuck,' Eva said. 'My cousin, Miss Copperfield, sent for a maid, but no one returned. What happened?'

The maid avoided Eva's eyes, and the hungry knot in Eva's stomach twisted into a knot of anxiety. 'Is Dora all right?'

'Yes, miss.'

'Then what happened? Why did no one come to help me? I sincerely hope that I don't have to report a forgetful domestic to my uncle. Did Dora ask you or the other maid to help?'

The maid's head snapped up, her cheeks flushed and her eyes wide. 'I was not allowed to open it for you.'

'Pardon?' Eva's fork stopped on the way to her mouth. 'Not allowed?'

'Mr Copperfield told me so, miss. He heard Miss Dora telling me to unstick the door and had a real strop, begging you pardon, but he did.' She looked thoroughly miserable. 'He told me not to bring food up, 'cos you might escape. But Miss Dora insisted I fetch you up some breakfast.'

'You mean I am a prisoner here?'

The maid nodded, her previously sulky expression now one of fear. 'I have to do as he says, else I'll lose my situation.'

Eva looked past the wan face of the girl to the landing. A quick dash past the maid and she could be out of the room. There must be some explanation. She raced for the door, flung it wide and careered into the looming figure of her uncle as he came down the corridor.

'So, my dear,' Jonas said, his face twisted with a mixture of amusement and menace. 'I take it you do not approve of my hospitality.' Confused, Eva staggered back. Jonas smiled coldly and looked at the quivering maid who now stood by the door. 'And you, miss, have disobeyed a very clear order.'

'Sir . . . '

'Go downstairs and back to the kitchens. I will not have disobedient staff. Be warned.'

The maid scampered off, leaving Eva alone to face her uncle.

'I have told the maids not to open the door and have ordered my daughter not to help you.'

'Why? What is this?' Eva had no choice but to back further into the room. Jonas stood outlined in the doorway, looming and dangerous.

'Do you really think that I am going to allow a slip of a girl, a runt of my brother's, to take away my home?'

'I'd not take it away,' Eva insisted. 'I told you I'd discuss it all. I have the papers, it's all legal.'

'Papers? What papers? Oh, those in your bag, do you mean? But you've lost it.'

Eva looked around and, to her horror, saw that the bag that she had left on the dressing table had gone.

'You sleep deeply,' Jonas said. 'It only took moments for my wife to slip the bag away. Now Fern Lodge is still mine. You'll have to stay here while I think what to do with you.'

Eva shuddered and took a breath. 'Please, Uncle. I wouldn't dream of taking your home. I knew nothing of all this until a few months ago. I didn't even know that my father had a brother. If we could just discuss this . . . '

Again, Jonas's voice cracked like a whip. 'I have no intention of discussing this or anything else my stupid brother might have done to spite me. When he left for America with your mother, he asked me to keep the Lodge. He was older only by a year, but I was much better able to maintain the estate.'

'I have a friend,' Eva said defiantly. 'Someone who will miss me and come searching.'

'Really? An Irish girl, I believe. Well, from what I made my daughter tell me, Miss Kelly won't be looking for you because you have not told her this address.'

Eva had expected to return to the convent's shelter and tell Niamh about Fern Lodge and her new-found family. She had not wanted to tell her about owning the house until it was all settled. Now she knew that Uncle Jonas was right. How could Niamh find her? A cold shudder slipped down her spine.

'I'll go. You can have the house; I have no need of it. Please, just free me.'

Jonas laughed. 'That would be foolish. No, I need to consider this problem. You can stay here until I have a solution.' He left the room, closing the door. Eva heard the key turn in the lock. She was trapped.

6

For two days Eva stayed trapped as a prisoner in the room, only seeing the maid who came to give her food and fresh water to wash in. Each time the maid came, Uncle Jonas was not far behind, hovering on the landing. No doubt he was waiting for Eva to try and escape.

It was on the third day that Eva's chance finally came. And she grabbed that chance fully. The maid came with breakfast, and Eva noticed at once that the girl seemed less tense than usual. Normally the girl was as jumpy as a cat, shooting looks over her shoulder at the looming figure of Jonas Copperfield. However, this morning she did not glance nervously or tremble.

Eva saw, to her delight, that her uncle was not there. It took only a moment to make her decision. With her back to

Eva, the maid was not aware when Eva silently snatched up her jacket from the peg on the door. The key was still in the outside lock. Eva ran, slammed the door and locked it, hearing surprised squeals from the room. She knew exactly where to go.

No one was around, but as Eva flew down the dark corridor, she could hear angry thumping coming from the room she had been locked in. The Forgotten Wing — that was where she would run to.

Flinging herself up the narrow stairway to the annex, Eva only stopped for breath when she had shut the door and pressed her hot forehead to the cool wood. Was she safe now? she wondered.

She didn't sleep much that night in the little bedroom. She had pushed the writing table against the door and jammed a chair under the handle, all the time wishing that the door still had a key. After spending a long time heaving the bed to the door as an extra weight to prevent it from opening, she had done all she could to stop anyone from getting in.

But then came the realisation that she had no idea what to do next. Eva decided that she would wait a day and let her uncle think she had escaped from the house altogether. Then during the night she would leave. But in the event, it was Dora who provided her escape.

Eva was glad of the morning. A central gasolier had been suspended over the table in the parlour and little lamps had been attached to the walls in the bedroom. But Eva had no idea if gas still reached this deserted part of the house, and was not certain of the condition of the lamps. More importantly, she did not want any light to seep under the door or through gaps in the curtains that would advertise her occupancy. Consequently, she had stumbled around in the cold darkness before finally curling up in an armchair and wrapping herself in her cloak and a blanket from the bed.

The little parlour overlooked the courtyard where laundry was hung out to dry, and cats bathed in patches of sunlight. A piece of muslin had been nailed across the window in an attempt to prevent soot from collecting on the glass. Eva tentatively peered out, careful not to be seen.

The sun was high, the cats dozing and the courtyard empty of people. One of Aunt Kathryn's little terriers wandered into the yard and snarled at a cat. The cat hissed, arched a long elegant back, and stalked off. Eva held her breath. Was her aunt nearby too, then? Pulling herself right against the wall, Eva peered cautiously out of the window, straining to keep herself as inconspicuous as she could.

It was only a matter of moments before a maid carrying a basket of wet washing came into the yard. Eva flung herself away from the window. She could hear the maid singing. Returning to the little bedroom, Eva chose a book and made her way back to the armchair in which she had spent a cold and uncomfortable night.

She must have nodded off, because she suddenly became aware of the door to the annex being banged and the handle rattled. She leapt out of the chair and stood rooted to the hideous carpet, trembling for fear of discovery.

Dora had said that no one came up here. Who then, was attempting to enter? It struck Eva that it must be Dora. She tiptoed to the door and pressed her ear to the wood. She could hear Dora muttering to herself in exasperation. Eva listened but could hear no one else.

'Dora?' Eva hissed.

'Who's there?' Dora sounded shocked. 'Eva? Is that you?'

'Shh! Yes, wait. I've jammed the door up. It'll take a bit of time for me to open it.'

Huffing and puffing, Eva eventually managed to drag the furniture away from the door. With her back aching and her breath coming in deep shivering rasps, Eva opened the door and grabbed her cousin's arm to drag her inside. Dora's eyes widened and she stumbled in, shocked.

'How did you . . . ? What . . . ?' Dora's words tumbled over each other and she gripped Eva's arms. 'I've been so worried.'

Quickly, Eva told her cousin how she had managed to escape from the room.

'We knew you'd gone, because the maid was locked in your room,' Dora said. 'My father tried to get me to tell him where you were, but of course I had no idea. The maid has lost her job, I'm afraid.'

Eva felt herself pale. 'I never intended for that to happen.'

'I think she's better off,' confided Dora. 'I wrote her a good recommendation. My parents refused to write a reference so I did. But we need to get you away from here. Wait until tomorrow. My parents are out all day visiting an elderly aunt in Crawley. I will plead a headache and not go. When they leave, you can escape.'

'But where will I go?'

Dora shrugged. 'Anywhere. Just away.'

'I have no idea where my bag is. Your parents took it. All the papers are there. Everything to prove that I am the owner of this house. I managed to look after it all the way from America, but now . . . '

Dora clutched at Eva's hands. 'But you must get away.'

'Back to London, I suppose.' Eva sighed. 'The shelter again.'

'My old schoolfriend's mother is looking for household help,' Dora mused.

'You mean a servant,' Eva answered wryly.

Dora flushed, but she smiled. 'Yes, but it is all I can suggest. I know that Lady Fleur is a fair woman. She is a widow. Her husband made money from the South African goldfields. The last maid left to work in a soap factory, apparently. She needs another maid.

You'll be able to get away from here until I find your bag, plus you'll have accommodation and money. My father would never think of looking for you as a servant.'

The plan seemed to be one that could be successful. Fern Lodge was not safe for Eva, and she was certainly not averse to hard work.

'My father won't have thrown out the papers, will he?' Dora looked worried.

'I hope not.'

Anxiously, Eva began to search in the old writing desk for paper and a pen. Finding some yellowed paper and a stubby pencil, she began to list the documents that Uncle Jonas had stolen and handed it to Dora. As her cousin scanned the list, Eva realised that there would need to be a long-term plan of action. She could not simply hide away in London while her inheritance slipped through her fingers.

Dora folded the list and put it in her bag. 'I shall come tomorrow after my parents have left. We can walk to the train station and from there catch a train to London. I shall accompany you. Let me write a reference for you and you can take it to Lady Fleur. If she does not offer you work — although I think she will — then write to me immediately at this address.'

Using another piece of paper and the little pencil, Dora wrote out an address in neat copperplate. 'I am a supporter of women's suffrage,' she explained. 'My mother and father are much against it, but I still sneak out to meetings. This is the address of my friend, Elizabeth Coral. She will get any note to me.' Here Dora grinned. 'She always manages to sneak details of meetings to me, and any news!'

Eva placed the note in her jacket pocket. 'Thank you.'

'You must be hungry,' Dora said. 'I'll bring you up some food and drink.'

'I'd be grateful. I can't thank you enough for your help.'

Giving her cousin a hug, Dora said,

'It's a pleasure to help you, Eva. Now, how does a pot of hot tea and some cake sound?'

★   ★   ★

As promised, Dora returned the next day. 'I have told Mother that I am suffering with lady's complaints. Mother refused then to let me go to our aunt's, saying it was 'unseemly' for me to do so.' She rolled her pretty dark eyes. 'Thank the Lord for a goose of a mother.'

'I am ready to go,' Eva said. 'Nervous, but ready. I hope it won't cause too much bother for you.'

'It is no bother at all,' Dora assured her cousin. 'But we must go now.'

The walk was filled with apprehension, and it was only when they arrived at the station that Eva began to believe she could truly escape her uncle. They did not have long to wait for a train, after purchasing their tickets to Crawley and then accepting a cup of tea from the stationmaster. The journey was uneventful, much to Eva's relief.

Once in Crawley, they had to wait for an hour for the next train to London. After more tea and a lot of nervous glances in case Dora saw anyone she knew, the cousins were relieved to get on the train and leave the town.

The train arrived in London, and Dora and Eva negotiated the underground trains to the shelter. Passing gaudy public houses and sad-eyed children, Eva realised how bleak and colourless London could be, especially after the Sussex countryside. Soot covered everything, blackening the buildings and tainting the air. Unpleasant smells from a nearby vinegar factory mingled with the odours of horses and grime.

Dora kept her skirt hem up off the ground, trying to avoid the dirt. 'I must say, I've never been to this part of the city before,' she said, screwing up her face against the filth.

They arrived at the Providence Night

Refuge, and Eva knocked on the door. A nun, smiling kindly, answered and asked if she could help.

'I had a room here a few nights ago,' Eva explained.

'I'm sorry, I don't quite remember . . .'

'With an Irish girl, Niamh Kelly,' Eva persisted.

'Oh, yes.' The nun nodded. 'I do recall now. That young lady secured a position as a maid somewhere. She didn't leave a forwarding address, I'm afraid. Do you still want a room?'

'Niamh's gone?' Eva felt her face blanch. 'No address? I'm surprised.'

'Oh, not many do leave one. I expect they feel there's no need. We've done our duty. Now, will both of you want a room?'

'It will just be me,' Eva said.

'I'll stay to help my cousin settle in,' Dora explained. 'I'm expected back today.'

'Step inside then.' The nun stood aside to allow Eva and Dora in. 'Now, how long do you think you'll need the room for? We can't give rooms indefinitely. We do try and help girls find work.'

'It will be for one night,' Eva told her. *I hope*, she added silently, mentally crossing her fingers that the reference from Dora would secure her a position with Lady Fleur.

After being shown to a room, Eva and Dora were left to their own devices.

'I can't believe that I'll never see Niamh again,' Eva said. 'We were good friends. I suppose she thought I'd not come back after I'd been gone for a few days. Maybe she thinks I was some fair-weather pal who never really valued our friendship.'

'It couldn't be helped,' Dora said softly. 'It was nothing you did. It was all my father's fault.'

Eva gave a weary sigh. 'I hope I can get that job.'

'Take the reference tomorrow,' Dora said. 'I'm sure you'll at least be interviewed. I'll get back and search for the papers. Write to me via Elizabeth — the address I gave you — as soon as you can.'

'I still have it.' Eva patted her jacket pocket where the paper was carefully folded. 'I hope we can sort everything out.' She tried to smile, but realised that she felt exhausted. Weariness had seeped into her bones, into the very fabric of her being.

She had had a difficult few weeks: her emigration, her nerves being taut as trip-wire while she'd been locked in her room at Fern Lodge, and now the uncertainty that lay ahead. In fact, Eva could not imagine anything more dear to her than sleep. The day had been arduous, and had taxed her to her limits.

Dora, too, seemed to be drooping. Her pretty dark eyes had become puffy and were tinged with bruise-like shadows.

'You need to get back home, Dora,' Eva said. 'I can never thank you enough for helping me.'

'My father has treated you shamefully,' her cousin said heatedly. 'I promise I'll do everything in my power to make it up to you.'

'But it wasn't your fault.'

'No, but I will make him see that he can't trample over people.'

'Take care, Dora,' Eva said, worried for her cousin.

'Oh, don't fret about me. I can manage my father; you see if I can't.'

7

Lady Fleur was looking at Eva as if seeing a very queer creature. Eva supposed that she looked delicate, and knew that her accent had an American twang to it, which must raise an interest in this woman.

Pushing a pile of letters and calling cards to one side, Lady Fleur rubbed the tips of her fingers over a weary brown. 'I am sorry that I seem a little . . . unready for our interview, but correspondence seems to take so long nowadays. Ever since my dear Arthur died . . . It was three years ago this winter, but still . . . I seem to have lost a part of me.' Straightening her back and smoothing away crumples on her dress, Lady Fleur peered at the reference that Dora had supplied. She seemed to shake herself free of melancholia and lent herself to the matter in hand. 'How is it, Miss Copperfield, that you are applying for a position as housemaid? Surely your family is above such a thing? You have no need for this, surely?'

Eva gave a small, tight smile. 'I have lived in America all my life. I did not even know that I had family here. I only found out a few months after my parents' accident. Then I came to England.'

'To find your father's family?' Lady Fleur prompted, sitting forward, her white hands pressed together.

'To claim my inheritance.'

'Oh?'

'Fern Lodge and its estates are mine. Left to me in my father's will.'

'Goodness!' The older woman sat back in surprise.

Eva explained about her parents' death and the subsequent poverty that she had had to endure. Out of respect to Dora, she did not mention her uncle locking her in the attic.

'My uncle is understandably concerned about my owning Fern Lodge,'

Eva said. 'I wish to make my own way in the world until my uncle can see a way to negotiating the problem.'

'A tricky situation. But as I am acquainted with the Copperfields and know Dora quite well, I will give you a job. You are a respectable young woman, and I think you have a stout heart within that slight frame. The terms are quite reasonable — twenty-three pounds a year, a fortnight's holiday each year, half day every Sunday, and a day and an evening off per month.'

'I hope my employment will be on the same terms as everyone else,' Eva insisted. 'Please don't favour me because you know my family.'

Giving Eva a smile, Lady Fleur promised, 'I would not insult you in such a way.'

Eva returned the grin. 'Then that's settled. But please, there is one more thing.'

'Yes?'

'Please don't tell my uncle or aunt

where I am. I would hate to get Dora into any bother.'

Lady Fleur became grim. 'Of course. I expect you need to sort things out before contacting your uncle again.'

Eva nodded, but refrained from adding that her uncle's determination to own Fern Lodge was likely to lead her into danger.

* * *

Eva soon settled into her life as a maid. She rose at six o'clock to draw up blinds, clean and dust the parlour, and set the fires. Her days were not easy, but she felt happy enough.

She had written to Dora as soon as she had moved into the house, but had received only one letter back, in which her cousin wrote how delighted she was that Eva had a job, and that she herself was still searching for the papers. After a week, Eva had had no other word from her. Had her cousin found the papers? Had her uncle disposed of them? As she made beds, swept stairs, and rubbed silver, she turned over her options. She realised soon enough that there was only one option: wait and have faith in Dora. Once Eva had decided on this, she felt a little more relaxed. Knowing that she could do nothing freed her from worrying about the problems she had encountered at Fern Lodge. She began to look forward to her day away from work.

'Where will you go?' her roommate Tilly asked the night before Eva's first day off. 'I usually go to my grandma's in Stepney. Take her some cake an' a few coins to see her right. Cook always lets me, you know. Soft really, despite appearances.'

'I'm not sure where to go,' admitted Eva, pulling the bedspread up and resting her head on the pillow with a sigh of thankfulness.

'Well, maids often go to the park,' mused Tilly. 'You could go an' see the boats on the Serpentine, have a coffee somewhere.'

'I suppose I'll just wander and have a look around London. I've not really had much time to see it.'

'Oh, well, you're not missing much.' Tilly threw her boots into one corner of the little attic room and snuggled down into her bed. 'I been here all me life an' I can't say as it's much to look at.'

Tilly was soon snoring, but Eva lay awake wondering whether to risk a train journey to Sussex. After puzzling over this, she decided that it would be too dangerous. She would have to be patient and wait for Dora to get the papers to her. She considered Tilly's suggestion about going to see the parks. Finally, she decided that that was what she would do.

★ ★ ★

The next day promised to be beautiful, and Eva looked forward to her outing. She dressed in a simple gown of autumnal brown and a wide hat of crushed velvet.

106

Placing a few coins in a drawstring purse, she made her way to Hyde Park. The sun shone bright on the Serpentine, the glassy man-made lake only disturbed by the oars of rowers. She people-watched for a while, but then her eye was caught by a figure strolling along a few yards in front of her.

Eva couldn't believe it at first, but she could not mistake the raven hair pinned up into curls and waves, or the swinging walk. It was Niamh! Holding up the hem of her dress, Eva tripped off across the grass towards her friend. After tapping the Irish girl on the shoulder, she was greeted first by large, surprised eyes, and then a wide grin.

'Eva!'

Enveloped in Niamh's hug, Eva felt a rush of happiness. It hadn't occurred to her before just how lonely she was. In New York she had never been lonely. Regular customers who patronised the coffee shop would often talk, discussing the meanderings of their lives as Eva polished copper and wiped spills from waxed tables. And when at the end of the day she trudged back to the damp riverside room, she would nod hellos to women balancing babies or bundles on their hips, and she'd smile at the inebriated tramp sprawled against mould-blackened walls. She was never without people to talk to. But here in London she spoke to no one apart from the other servants of Lady Fleur. Niamh's friendship was most welcome.

'I thought you were in Sussex,' Niamh said, easily sliding her hand into the crook of Eva's arm.

'Well . . . ' She began to tell Niamh her story, watching as various expressions puckered or creased Niamh's features — anger, surprise, concern.

'You've really been though the mill, haven't you, Eva?'

'You could say that,' Eva answered wryly.

'Is Lady Fleur good to you, though?'

'Oh yes.' Eva could not fault her employer. 'Very fair.'

She suddenly realised that she had not enquired after Niamh's own circumstances. Certainly she was looking very well. 'That's enough about me. How are you doing?'

'You never saw such a place,' the Irish girl enthused. 'So grand, and so many servants! I'm just under-parlourmaid, but the people are good to me. And . . . ' Here her bright eyes sparkled. 'Joe — from the ship — he's workin' as a costermonger at the markets. Selling veggies. Trying to make his money to go back to his da's farm.'

Seeing the look on her friend's face gave Eva a pang of emotion as she remembered Ben. Where was he now? she wondered.

Linking arms, Eva and Niamh walked along the well-kept paths of the park, watching people and chatting. Eva became aware of a small group of ladies, genteel and finely dressed, who had congregated at the edge of Rotten Row. Two were in a landau with gleaming horses, and three younger girls stood by, twittering like excited robins. All five had large-brimmed silk hats, shading fair and unspoilt complexions. It appeared that they were looking up the Row at the various riders and carriages.

'It *is* him,' one of the girls in the carriage said, her red curls frizzing round a white heart-shaped face.

'You thought that yesterday.' Her driving companion peeked out from underneath the purple silk of her hat. She was tiny, and her bonnet was much too large for her dark head.

'Yes,' giggled another girl. 'It was Lord Pallister! How you could mistake him for Lord Charrington, I can't think. Benjamin Charrington is such a beau!'

The redhead flushed and lowered her eyes. 'I suppose at a distance it seemed they were one and the same. Their horses are, I believe, from the same stock.'

The girls chirped on merrily, but Eva had already grown bored of this simple gossip. She turned to Niamh, who had been watching a girl throw a ball to a golden Saluki puppy.

'Do you think we'll ever moon and sigh over some flash lord?' she said, laughing. 'Poor things! They have no idea what's coming!'

Niamh kicked gently at the puppy's ball that had rolled near her feet. 'Those girls are talking about Lord Charrington. To be sure, he's the most eligible fellow this Season, so he is. I've never seen him myself, of course, but the maid that answers the door has, and she says he's a pleasure to look at and to talk to. Mind you, she's a saucy thing and no mistake. But if this Lord Charrington is as good as people say, it'd be worth catching an eyeful, eh, pet? But I doubt he's such a dream as these sparrows say. All these society men all look the same to me.'

A warm breeze started up as the two friends watched the trio of riders cantering towards them, the three-beat thrumming of well-shod hooves becoming louder.

'It *is* Lord Charrington!' a thin twig of a girl exclaimed as the riders closed nearer.

'Here's our man.' Niamh frowned into the sun to watch the riders. 'I wonder which one he is?'

Eva sighed at the insipid gossip, but looked up anyway. Her heart stopped for a few beats, then hammered wildly at her ribs. Resplendent in navy-blue riding apparel, atop a fine chestnut mount that tossed a proud head, was none other than Ben from the *Baltic*.

Eva felt her heart flip. She knew that she was staring, but it was only when Ben's eyes met hers that she shook herself and felt heat flood through her. She lowered her gaze and swallowed.

'Good Lord!' explained Niamh. ''Tis your Ben!'

'He's not 'my Ben',' Eva snapped. Then she felt ashamed of herself for being so rude. She gripped Niamh's arm. 'I'm sorry, it's just that . . . I'm not sure what to make of it.' She risked raising her eyes to Ben once more.

He had jolted his horse back into movement. Eva watched the trio of riders retreat and felt her mind skid to a halt.

She later realised, when she got back to Lady Fleur's, that she could hardly remember the journey back or much of what Niamh had said to her. She was too bewildered. All she knew was the painful beating of her heart and a longing to unravel the mystery surrounding the man she had been thinking of ever since setting eyes on him.

She decided to take a bath. Lady Fleur encouraged both cleanliness and health in her staff and so allowed for warm baths each week. The warm water soaked over Eva's tired body.

The shock of seeing Ben, dressed in all his finery, parading around Hyde Park and calling himself a lord . . .

She had been right all along. Ben was a charlatan. He must be — how else could he have gone from steerage passenger to lord? But on the other hand, those silly, vapid girls gossiping and mooning about like ducks had been very clear that he was this Lord Charrington. Even Niamh had heard of him. Eva would certainly love to hear his story!

Soaping herself and trying to relax into the scent of lavender, Eva willed her mind to turn to other thoughts. She tried to distract herself by thinking about her employment. Lady Fleur was a kindly employer who always kept her staff stocked with the things they needed, and always treated servants with respect. Eva knew that she was lucky. There were many in the upper echelons of society who cared little, if anything, for their staff.

Eva considered the twists of fate that had led her to this. A maid at a fancy London address! It was still a far cry from being mistress of Fern Lodge, as she rightfully was, but at least she was safe. It had, of course, not been her first thought to want the house and all that came with it. But since Jonas had treated her so wickedly, she had decided to exercise her rights. She'd let him and his family live there, but it would now be on her terms. How dare he think to bully her, his daughter, and his servants? She would teach him a lesson.

Ownership of the house was still within her reach, if Dora could manage to find the papers. Eva had worried that her uncle would destroy the documents, but then she realised that Jonas was no fool. He would not reduce to ashes anything that others might know about — and at least two solicitors knew of the will and the accompanying paperwork. Her uncle would not want to be seen as a liar and a criminal. He'd have a plan. And Eva needed to try and second-guess it.

As she dried herself and put on her cambric nightdress, Eva considered the odd situation. Wearily, she climbed into the little truckle bed. Tilly was fast asleep, little snores emanating from beneath the cornflower-blue candlewick bedspread. Eva tried to still her mind. There would be answers soon; she just had to be patient.

8

Cook fluttered about, adding butter and spices to the chicken pie. Tilly was fussing over boiling up the wine, ginger and cloves for the jelly wine sauce. Eva had swept and raked the stoves, having been up since five that morning, black-leading and polishing the iron-work.

The week before the party had been the busiest Eva had known since working for Lady Fleur. The flagstones around the house were scrubbed, windows cleaned, tables scoured, and even the boot scraper by the door was black-leaded now. She was so tired that as she slumped into bed, there did not seem to be one part of her that did not ache. But she had had praise aplenty from Cook and Lady Fleur. It was now the day of the party, and everyone seemed to be in a lather.

'Oh, it's been so long since the mistress had a party that I'm all a-dither,' Cook complained as she wiped a floury hand across her forehead. 'Don't you let that sauce catch, Tilly, or *I'll* catch *you!*'

Tilly pulled a face and grinned at Eva. 'It's all in hand, don't fret.'

'Cheeky.' Cook tutted. 'You just keep an eye on it.'

Having seen the menu, Eva certainly felt for the cook. The courses were fashionable and intricate. What with plovers, lemon water ices and lobster, poor Cook was running herself quite ragged.

'Oh Eva, go and finish the table, there's a dear. The silver has been polished, just set it out.'

With an eager step, Eva made her way upstairs. The room looked lovely, and Eva quickly set to placing the shining cutlery on the table. Cards of stiff ivory had been embossed in gold lettering with the names of guests. Eva read them as she went. None of them, of course, she knew, until she came to one at the corner of the long table: '*Lord Benjamin Charrington*'.

Her breath caught and her insides flipped. Ben was to be a guest here? It was not such a total surprise, she considered, after the first initial jolt of shock. After all, wasn't everyone saying that he was one of the most eligible men, and one of the most sought-after guests of the Season? She finished setting out the cutlery, picked up two crystal vases from the side table, and made her way back to the scullery to arrange the flowers.

'You look miles away, Eva,' Cook commented when Eva returned. 'Quite peaky, if you was to ask me.'

'Perhaps a little tired,' Eva murmured.

'Well, the Season's always a big thing. You'll get used to it. Now, madam's called up for another pot of tea and some scones. They're on the side. Take 'em up, Eva, please.'

Lady Fleur had either been bustling

119

about or locked in deep consultations with her lady's maid and dressmaker. Eva took the pot of tea to her mistress's room, where Lady Fleur was trying on a close-fitting tailored dress the colour of a clear sky.

'Eva, what do you think?'

Astounded at being asked for her opinion, Eva stuttered over her words. 'It's ... I think ... it's beautiful, madam.'

'Mm, well, I'm not sure I like the colour.'

The dressmaker rolled her eyes and tugged and primped at the silk. 'It suits you wonderfully. It shows your enviable shape.'

Lady Fleur turned to Eva once more. 'My dear, do you agree?'

'I'm not so sure about fashions. Maybe American ones, but not English. But I can say that the colour does look well on you.'

Still not looking totally convinced, Lady Fleur turned back to the mirror. 'Well, it will have to do. It is too late now. And Miss Finch has put in so much work. I'll never find such a good dressmaker as her.'

Miss Finch blushed prettily and looked pleased.

'Now, my hair. I think I shall wear the pearl tiara and the large feather. Yes?'

Both the dressmaker and maid murmured agreement and set about arranging Lady Fleur's blonde curls into a fashionable coiffure. Eva placed the tray on the table, returned to the kitchen and relayed the drama over the dress.

'She worries,' pointed out Cook as she selected the best specimens from a tub of potatoes. Clicking her tongue in exasperation, she threw aside those she deemed unacceptable. 'The Season means she has to entertain. And, of course, she has to be entertained.'

Tilly frowned up at Cook, her head bobbing like a bird's. 'Why worry, though? It must be grand to go to those parties an' dance an' all.'

'She needs new clothes for each do and needs to keep her house looking good. It's what these rich folk do.'

Selecting a stiff-bristled brush and a terracotta pot from a shelf, Tilly said, 'No! She don't have to have a new dress each time, surely? And the house always looks nice.'

Cook waved a peeling knife at the girl. 'Of course she needs a new frock each time, else folk'll say as she's poor. How can she be seen in the same dress twice?'

'*I* have to,' Tilly pointed out.

Laughing, Eva said, 'Tilly, you are not expected to look grand. Lady Fleur needs to look like she can afford many clothes.'

'Then she should do what my ma taught me — get a needle an' thread and change her frock. A ribbon here, a frill there, take off that bit of lace . . . I'd do it for her, I'm good with thread.'

'You're a cheeky mare, Matilda Blackstock,' scolded Cook. 'Mind yer manners an' talk about your mistress with respect. She can't go round in patched-up gowns. The very idea!'

Tilly shrugged. 'I just can't see the point. I'm not being rude.'

'Well, those potatoes won't peel themselves. All of those are good.' With a wave of her hand, Cook indicated a pile put aside. 'And after that, you can chop some parsley. It'll be nothing less than a miracle if I get this all ready in time.'

* * *

The party had started well. Tilly was mooning about, starry-eyed at all the finery she saw about her.

'I shall have to nip into the garden for more herbs,' Cook said after giving Tilly a dozen scoldings for not concentrating. 'You can't remember a thing I've taught you today, Matilda. As if I don't have enough to do. You wash those pans — and Eva, please fetch the used glasses and replace them with clean goblets.' Cook bustled off into the garden, throwing her shawl over her shoulders and muttering crossly.

Eva went to the dining room. The ladies wore dresses of all hues. She sighed and tried to imagine what it must be like to float along on a cloud of calm, not having any worries. Eva's own concerns could not, however, be altered by money. Her papers were still missing and she was becoming desperate to hear from Dora, concerned that she might be in some danger by colluding with Eva and helping her escape. Eva sighed again as she heard tinkling laughter.

Brushing a hand over the black skirt of her formal work dress, and adjusting the white cap, she turned to go back to the kitchen. Balancing a silver tray with empty champagne flutes, she picked her way carefully down the back stairs to the kitchen. These stairs were unlit and uncarpeted, and Eva was always afraid of tripping on the flagstone steps.

Upon nearing the kitchen, Eva could hear voices. She could not make out what was being said, but one of the voices was most certainly a man's, deep and rich. Frowning, Eva pushed open the door with her hip and entered. Gasping, she reeled back from what she saw.

Ben was standing with his head close to Tilly's, holding her hand and smiling down into her kittenish face. Tilly laughed at something Ben murmured to her and Eva watched as Ben brought the girl's hand to his lips.

'How could you?' Eva spat out the words with disgust.

Tilly leapt away like a cat caught on a fire. 'Oh, Eva, you . . . '

'Eva?' The emotions that chased across Ben's face were enough to tell Eva that he had not forgotten her. 'I thought you were in Sussex. You said you had family there.'

Her head high, Eva looked daggers at him. 'I do, although I don't see it's your business. More to the point, what are you doing to poor Tilly?'

But Ben brushed this off and said, 'I never thought to see you again. I can't tell you how happy I am. Only I do wish you'd tell me what happened since we parted on the ship.'

'I'm not interested in a rake like you.'

'Eva, please don't,' Tilly begged.

'Don't worry, Tilly.' Eva's temper had been roused and she was prepared to use any manner at her disposal to protect the poor maid. 'I hold nothing against you. It's this piece of flotsam that must be held accountable!'

'Oh, but Eva, you must listen to me . . . ' Tilly had paled and she looked wildly from Ben to Eva and back again.

Crashing the tray on the nearest surface, Eva stamped over to the bemused Ben. 'Sir, I think you have overstepped the mark here. It's one thing to go gadding about posing as a lord, but quite another to push your vile and unwanted attentions on a poor innocent girl.'

Tilly gave a little squeak and clutched

at Eva's arm with small twig-like fingers.

'And you, Eva Copperfield,' hissed Ben, 'had better learn to listen and amass all the facts before letting loose that formidable temper. Don't you know that a show of the tantrums will crease that pretty face?'

As Tilly scampered from the kitchen, Eva, speechless with anger at his audacity, lifted up a ladle and aimed it at Ben. To her surprise and annoyance, he caught it deftly and placed it back on its hook. He then turned to her, his features as calm as summer water.

'Miss Copperfield, I think I owe you an explanation. If you could just refrain from trying to knock me senseless with kitchen utensils for a minute, I will gladly enlighten you.'

Breathing hard, her chest straining, she steadied herself by gripping the long wooden table. Ben stood but a foot away from her. She was aware, too aware, of the sweep of his lashes and the broad expanse of his shoulders.

'I *am* Lord Charrington.' It was said calmly, but Eva could see a thin vein pulsing in his forehead. This was causing him some emotion, although like a true Englishman he was keeping the flames of feeling damped down.

'You were in steerage,' Eva accused. 'As poor as I was.'

'Oh, Eva.' He reached out a hand, but she stepped back. Her instincts screamed to move towards him. Her heart yelled to be pulled into his orbit and spun round at his will, but she would not let it happen. He was a liar, possibly even a criminal, and — from what Eva had seen of his behaviour towards Tilly — a cad.

Eva snapped her eyes shut for a brief moment, gathered her thoughts, and kept herself at arm's reach. 'You have no excuse,' she said. 'Don't even try to deny what anyone can see.'

'It was a bet. The gentlemen with whom I was travelling had wagered that I would not manage the trip in third class. I am a lord; I live like one. But I am no dandy. I was willing to spend two weeks holed up in conditions I have never even dreamt of.'

Eva screwed up her nose. 'To all your sins you willingly add 'gambler'.'

Ben laughed. 'Yes, if you wish to put it like that. But my own purse never benefited.'

Eva snorted her disbelief.

'I am patron of a charity that houses unfortunates and their children. Homeless women can come and be fed and given shelter. Their children have safe beds and good food. The money I made from my wager went to the home. I never saw a penny. Indeed, I never needed any of it.'

Eva wanted to believe him so badly that the taste of it stuck in her mouth. But she was confused. 'What about Tilly?'

'Tilly?' His countenance registered confusion until a light dawned and he smiled. 'Little Matilda Blackstock? Her mother was a poor woman, fallen on that saddest of occupations to pay for her child's food and warmth. They came to the home. Matilda's mother died of a fever and Matilda was helped to find this position here. I even managed to help her find her maternal grandmother, who was more than willing to take her in until she got the position as maid.'

Was Ben speaking the truth? Eva imagined the poor woman, forced to sell her body and her dignity to help her child live.

'Matilda's mother was one of the first women to find shelter at the charity. I keep in touch with all the women and their children as far as I humanly can.'

'You still lied to me.'

'What would you have thought of me, eh? A mad lord slumming it? I could not have that. Besides, part of the bet was that no one should know or guess the truth. I'd have lost if I'd told you, although I was desperate to.'

Eva was painfully aware that they were alone in the scullery. Ben's clothes were of a fine cut and cloth; she wore the practical but drab uniform of a maid. She was reminded that when they had met on the boat she hadn't thought him a third-class passenger. But then she had envisaged the steerage men to be of hardworking, rough-handed stock and had thought Ben a charlatan, a trickster. Now, although plausible, she did not want to be gulled by his explanation.

'You had better get on with whatever it is that lords do,' she said testily. 'I doubt they spend their time sneaking about in kitchens and sculleries kissing maids.'

'No?' Suddenly Eva was pulled into an embrace, and his warm lips were seeking hers. The kiss sent a wave of emotion over her; she was drowning in it. When he pulled away, still gripping her arms, her head swam for a moment and she stood gazing at him. Then snapping herself back, she fought the urge to slap him.

'How dare you!' she spluttered.

'I dare,' he answered jauntily. 'I just

wanted you to know that lords can sneak into sculleries and kiss maids. And don't pretend to be shocked or offended. You must know that I have been meaning to do that ever since I spotted you watching me in New York harbour. In fact, I've thought of nothing but you since then.'

Such was the shock of this bold statement that Eva simply watched Ben, 'Lord Charrington', leave, and could find no wit in her to reply.

* * *

'They will need the ballroom soon,' Cook said. 'Just make sure the curtains are drawn and the candelabras are lit.'

Eva made her way to the room set aside as a ballroom. The carpet had been rolled back to reveal the varnished floor. Pulling the curtains shut, she watched as the band began to set up their instruments. Lady Fleur had hired a string quartet, and Eva was soon drawn into the lovely music as she made her way around the room, lighting candles, closing curtains and plumping cushions on the chairs and chaise longues that had been placed for those who wished to rest between dances.

She was still in turmoil about Ben's treatment of Tilly as she made her way back down the corridor towards the scullery and kitchen. Had he spoken the truth? So distracted was she that she did not notice the figure moving from the other end of the corridor until they nearly collided. Her insides turned to water when she saw it was Ben.

'So we meet again, Miss Copperfield.' He looked resplendent in his jacket the colour of deep red wine.

Eva shuddered, a shiver born from the nearness of him. 'I have nothing to say to you,' she said coolly, her heart a bird with wings beating against her chest.

'Oh Eva,' he sighed. 'Do you really still believe that I am some debauched lord? Some wicked cad? You must — '

'Stop!' Eva cried, holding up her hands as if to push him away.

'Do you hear the music?' Ben asked softly.

'Of course I do,' she snapped.

'A waltz. Do you remember the *Baltic*?'

How could she forget? She recalled the feel of his hands as he held her. Her body remembered everything about his touch as they had danced in the General Room of the ship. How long ago that seemed now.

'We could dance now.' Ben held out a hand, but Eva stepped away.

'I can't,' she whispered.

'I apologise for kissing you. Ah, well, no, that is not strictly true. I cannot apologise for that, because I am not sorry I showed you my feelings. But I apologise for upsetting you.'

'I really have nothing more to say to you, my lord.'

'You don't want to dance?'

'I don't. Not in the corridor and not with you.'

Exasperated, Ben ran his hand

through his ash-brown hair. 'I have explained all that.'

'I'm not sure I believe you.'

Ben was just about to speak when they heard the tapping of boot heels along the corridor.

'Ah, Lord Charrington.' Lady Fleur appeared round the corner. At seeing Eva, she gasped. 'Eva! What are you doing here? My dear Benjamin, I do apologise. My staff should be downstairs. But the girl is new to London and this is her first position. Please do not take unkindly to this lapse. I assure you she did not mean any offence.'

Eva's cheeks flamed red and she cast her eyes downward. How could she have committed such a faux pas? Servants were meant to be invisible.

'My dear Fleur,' said Ben kindly, 'please don't worry. She has done nothing untoward. In fact it is I who stopped her. I have misplaced a glove and merely asked her if she had seen it.'

Eva's soul leapt. He had come to her defence!

'However, she has not, so I must hope it turns up.' Ben bowed to Lady Fleur. 'Please accompany me back to the ballroom. I believe the dancing is about to begin, and I insist on having the first dance with you, dear Fleur.'

The two went off, leaving Eva to slump against the wall. What on earth to make of him? He grew more complicated than ever.

* * *

'Tilly? Lord Charrington — who . . . I mean, how do you know him?'

It was past two in the morning, and Eva and Tilly had crawled into their beds. Tilly's eyelids were already drooping as she peered wearily at Eva.

'Lord Charrington?'

'Yes. That business in the kitchen.'

Her eyes now wide, Tilly heaved herself up onto her elbow. 'Eva, that ain't what it looked like, I swear.'

'He explained, but I'm not sure I believed him.'

'I've known him since I were a little nipper. Me ma was poor an' he helped us.'

Eva's heart thumped.

'It was him what got me this job,' Tilly continued.

'So what he said was true? The home, the charity?'

Snuggling back down under the covers and yawning, Tilly murmured, 'Yes. I told you it weren't nothing off. I'm a good girl.'

Eva pulled the candlewick cover up to her chin. 'Thank you, Tilly.' But Tilly had already fallen asleep.

9

The next time that both Eva and Niamh had a day off, they met in the Lyon's Corner House on Regent's Street. It was a most dramatic building, laid out like a ballroom, although despite its fancy décor, it served all types of customers. To Eva's surprise, Niamh seemed quite at home, even waving happily to the white-capped waitresses.

The food was homely and cheerful. The girls sat beneath the glass chandeliers and made inroads into sweet tea and cakes. Eva watched outside as dusty little sparrows darted from nooks and crannies, and then she began to tell Niamh about her encounter with Ben.

'He told me he really is Lord Charrington,' she said, stirring a sugar lump into her tea until it dissolved. 'He said that he was in steerage for a bet. The money was to go to a charity that he'd set up for homeless women and children.'

Niamh looked thoughtful. 'I think it might just be the truth.'

'I . . . I have to say, I think I believe him too.' Eva couldn't quite work out what her feelings were. She certainly *wanted* to believe him.

Chewing thoughtfully on her teacake, Niamh still sported a frown. After she had finished, she said, 'I suppose there's no harm trying to find out once and for all.'

'How do you mean?'

'Well, you could go to his house.' Here her eyes brightened and she looked strangely pleased with herself.

Eva saw a major drawback to this idea. 'I don't know where he lives, do I, Niamh?'

'I do.' Niamh beamed. She sat back and dabbed her napkin at a smudge of butter on her lip. 'I was asked to run an errand. I had a bit of time, so I took meself off for a walk to see Buckingham Palace. On the way, I saw Ben — 'Lord Charrington' — at one of the big fancy houses. He didn't recognise me from the ship. A footman let him in.'

'It could have been a friend's house,' Eva objected. 'He didn't use a key?'

'Posh folks don't always. Anyway, I heard him say to the footman, 'I'll take luncheon in my study.' Must be his house if it's his study and he's givin' orders to the footman.'

Eva had to agree. She asked Niamh to describe the house. Niamh could not remember the number, but she said that it had distinctive black and gold railings and a sphynx-like statue at the front door. Eva felt sure she could find it.

After finishing the pleasant cream tea, the friends prepared to go their separate ways. 'Be careful, pet,' warned Niamh as she adjusted her hat. 'It's a queer craic, this. I'll not have you hurt, so I won't.'

With a smile that hid her own

apprehension, Eva said breezily, 'I'll be fine.'

'Yes, well make sure you are.' Niamh shook her head, tiny curls dancing at her forehead. 'What am I going to do with you?'

Eva was wrapped in a warm hug, and then Niamh left. Eva dallied for a few moments before hardening her resolve. She took a deep breath and made up her mind. She was going to see Ben.

*   *   *

After the party thrown by Lady Fleur, Eva had thought of little else but the kiss Ben had given her. She grew warm with a million conflicting emotions as she relived it. She had been shocked, yes, but also exhilarated, and to some extent extremely flattered that he had felt that way about her. Yet in another breath she admonished herself for allowing him to govern her emotions. Hadn't she seen him with Tilly? Hadn't her eyes told her that Ben was low in morals?

Yes, indeed her eyes had told her, but her heart hadn't been so sure. And Ben had given an explanation that was plausible. Eva allowed these thoughts to chase themselves like puppies after their tails. Such was her confusion that she decided not to go to find him after all. She needed a clearer head.

Now, on her next day off, she had once more gone to the park. She was to meet Niamh and had arrived a good half-hour early. She slowly made her way to the Row, watching a well-dressed lady ride past, elegant and aloof. It occurred to her that there was a good chance that Ben would be riding, and realised that she had absolutely no idea what she would do or say if she did see him again.

After nearly twenty minutes of watching and listening to the gossip of those beside her, Ben had not yet appeared. Maybe this was foolish. Eva was about to turn and go to meet Niamh when she saw the shimmering gloss of a chestnut mount coming towards her. Ben. Heart beating wildly, Eva made herself watch as he rode on.

He neared her and their eyes met. She couldn't help but notice the surprised raise of his eyebrow and the pleased look on his handsome face. She lowered her gaze but was aware that he had pulled his horse over to her. She raised her head, aiming to look aloof.

'Eva, how pleasant.' He removed his glove and extended a hand.

Eva shook it briefly. 'Lord Charrington,' she greeted stiffly. 'I see you have found your gloves. Yet another lie.'

He smiled at her asperity and nodded. 'How pleasant for you to be out on such a fine day. And I am pleased that you are grateful for my little fib. It no doubt saved you a scolding.'

Eva cringed at her stupidity. 'I do thank you.'

'Good. Then I wonder if you would accompany me for a walk?'

'I . . . I'm not sure that would be permitted.'

'By whom? We can walk, surely? Propriety is all very well, but it does rather get in the way of a friendship, don't you think?'

Eva was startled. 'Friendship? Is that what you consider our acquaintance to be? How gratifying.' She tried to sound derisive and harsh, but was sure she simply sounded petty.

After eyeing Eva with curiosity, Ben said, 'You don't consider it so, Miss Copperfield?'

'I don't suppose I know you well enough for it to be more than a . . . an association. Besides, you are a lord and I am a mere housemaid.'

'Ah,' Ben said, now all mischief and twinkling eyes. 'So you agree then that I am a lord?'

Eva bushed furiously, and her tongue tripped over her speech as she found herself embarrassed and flustered. 'Well, that is what you say you are. Are you saying you aren't?'

'I am relieved that you finally believe me.'

'I never quite said that!'

'Eva, let us walk. We can get away from wagging tongues and flapping ears.' Ben took her hand and slipped it into the crook of his arm. 'We can trifle and dally with clever words and twisting around what each other has said until we are caught up in knots. I don't want to do that. I would like to talk about pleasant things.'

'Oh, like what, for instance?' Eva felt she had no choice but to allow herself to be led where Ben was going.

'You.' He became softer and he smiled down at her. 'I have thought about nothing else but you . . . ah, but I have already told you that.'

'What is it you want, Ben? I really don't feel like being messed about. I value honesty, you know.'

'Ah, my dear Eva. So do I.' He stopped and looked over the Serpentine. 'So tell me, I beg you — what has happened to you since arriving in

145

England? I had imagined you safe in the bosom of your family, yet I find you here a maid.'

His voice was warm velvet. Eva felt her throat constrict. How she wanted him to kiss her again, yet she dreaded him doing so. 'What does it matter?'

'It matters because I care.' He took hold of her hand and held it in a light, gentle grip. 'Tell me.'

Eva took a breath and began to tell him about her uncle. It felt good to unburden herself, and yet at the same time she felt that she must not open up to Ben. She was, by rights, an heiress. But until she gained Fern Lodge, she was stuck as a maid. No lord could love or marry a servant.

'I will help,' Ben said, when Eva had finished her story.

Eva removed her fingers from his and tilted her chin with an air of defiance. 'I am fine. I don't need any help.'

'I am not favoured by you, am I?' He spoke quietly, an air of sadness tinting his words. He turned to her. 'Maybe this should be the end then. If you still think badly of me and I cannot change your mind . . . ' He sighed, took her hand and lightly kissed her trembling fingers. 'I shall not compromise you any more. Let this be a parting of the ways; although, as Shakespeare so mournfully wrote, it will be sweet sorrow.'

'I am sure you are right, Lord Charrington,' Eva answered crisply, willing her voice not to shiver as much as her body. 'It seems we are at odds, and therefore I can only see this as an end.'

Ben bowed over her hand then nodded. 'I shall return to my horse.' He turned on his heel and strode off.

Eva willed him to turn back while praying he wouldn't. Then, just as strongly, she willed herself not to cry. What madness was this?

* * *

'Ah, there you are, Eva.' Lady Fleur looked radiant in a loose tea gown the

147

colour of dusky pink roses. 'I have an errand for you, if Cook can spare you?'

Eva was wiping down the paintwork and skirting in the ballroom before the carpet was rolled back into place. She stood, aware of the ache in her legs where she had been kneeling for too long. 'I can ask Cook, madam.'

'Good. Now, I have an account with Harrods. They sent a large hamper for the ball, and I want you to go and pay. Cook has the money. She knows the ins and outs of it all.'

Eva curtsied and said that she would go and speak to Cook. The woman huffed a little at being without Eva for a while, but agreed that she should go if that was what Lady Fleur had requested.

As Cook bustled about preparing a chicken, Eva pulled on her jacket and pocketed the money for the hamper.

'Now I'll let you out and lock the door,' Cook said, wiping her hands on her apron. 'Come on, and be careful. You have a tidy sum of money there,

Eva. Go straight to the shop.'

As she stepped outside, the sun shed light and warmth on her face, and she stretched aching limbs and enjoyed the walk. She had not walked for many minutes when she heard a purring rumble.

Glancing back, she saw a car. Automobiles still made her feel uneasy. She had never been inside one and the thought of riding in a 'horseless carriage' was not pleasant. Still, rich people had them now, and she supposed this driver was going slowly so as to show off his employer's taste in transport.

To her surprise though, the car stopped and the driver stepped out. He was as sleek as the car itself and made his way towards her.

'Miss Copperfield?' he asked in a voice that oozed smoothness.

Her surprise must have been evident, because his face twisted into a sneer that sent Eva's hackles rising. 'Oh yes, Miss Copperfield. I know all about you.'

'Then I'm sorry, sir, but it seems you have the advantage of me.' Eva's stomach turned painfully.

'True, true.' He nodded and moved closer, the scent of his cologne stinging her nostrils. His eyes were as cold and hard as pebbles. He suddenly grabbed at her arm. 'May I suggest that you get in the car? I don't want any fuss.'

Eva thought of kicking, yelling, biting; anything to call attention to what was happening. But instead she found herself frozen with fear.

'You are needed elsewhere,' her captor hissed. His scrawny frame belied his strength. Looking for the entire world as if he were a noble and considerate chauffeur helping a lady into the car, he guided her to the back seat, his fingers like crab's pincers.

'You don't need to hold me like that,' Eva seethed. 'I have no intention of going anywhere. It seems I have no choice in the matter anyway.'

The car door slammed shut and soon they had pulled away. Their destination was a quiet cul-de-sac in what Eva later learnt was St John's Wood. The villa was what could be described as bijou, looking like a child's drawing of a house, with a door, four windows and squat red roof.

After being hauled out of the car, Eva was roughly pushed in front. She had little choice but to stumble into the villa. 'What is this?' she demanded. 'I take it this is my uncle's doing?'

Her kidnapper shrugged. 'Couldn't say. I just get paid.'

'How did you find me?'

'I had a description and an address.'

Eva frowned. How on earth could this man have gained her address? Then she realised that it must have been from the letter she'd written to Dora. Her uncle must have been through Dora's things and discovered her whereabouts!

'You have a room waiting for you.'

She was shown to an upstairs room and once again imprisoned. Would her uncle never give up? She slumped on the bed and sighed. As she did so, she heard the crackle of paper.

With a sickening feeling, she remembered the money that she had been given to take to Harrods. What if Lady Fleur thought she had run away with it? She hated to think that her employer might think badly of her. Eva vowed to keep the money safe whatever happened.

10

'We're going now, Dora.' Kathryn pulled on her silk gloves, fastening the delicate pearl buttons at the wrist. 'I do wish you'd come. You need to socialise. This is a backwater as it is. It isn't like London. You meet people in London. Here there are so few people worthy of meeting, especially eligible men.'

Her mother's snobbery irritated Dora. She had no wish to go anywhere that involved meeting eligible men. 'I'm finishing my correspondence. You always tell me it's good to keep up with letters.'

Kathryn sniffed with derision. 'You will be an old maid. I really do think we should arrange a coming-out for you. Although it would require a lot of hard work.' She glided from the room — elegant, beautiful, and cold as stone.

Dora waited until she could hear the car engine start. Then, when she could no longer detect the crunch of wheels on gravel, she rushed to Jonas's study. She had found the study key left in the door only a few days ago. Her father was usually so careful about locking the room that it had been like a gift. She had rushed in and rummaged in the desk drawer, finding a spare key beneath papers and old letters. She had taken it, hoping to use it at a later date, hoping her father would not miss it.

Now, with trembling fingers, she unlocked the study door and slipped into the room. As far as she could see, the papers were not in the desk drawer. Eva had told her to look for a brown envelope. Dora searched, panic rising like bile. Just as she was about to give up, she felt the bottom of the drawer give way.

Shocked that she had broken it, she tried to replace the wooden slat, until she realised that it was actually a false bottom. And lying underneath it was the envelope! She grabbed it and quickly flicked through the contents. She would have to check them against the list Eva had given her. Tidying up the desk and drawer, leaving it as it had been, Dora went back to her room. She locked her door and pulled out letters and deeds, sighing with unrestrained relief. The papers were all there!

Dora pushed them into a bag and covered them with a silk shawl in case anyone should see inside. Her hands shook as she did so. Despite her tenacity, Dora had never really gone against her father's wishes before. But Jonas Copperfield's behaviour was too much, beyond the pale. How could he have done this? Kidnapping his own niece!

With weak knees and beating heart, Dora grabbed the bag and left the house before she could be stopped.

* * *

'Miss Copperfield,' squeaked Cook. 'Surely you should have come through the main entrance. You're a family friend!'

'I need to speak to Eva,' Dora explained.

Cook's face contorted, and she folded her arms across her chest as if ready for a long session of venting annoyed steam. 'Mm, wouldn't we all?'

Dora was confused. Tilly sidled up and said, 'Eva went out two days ago. She ain't been seen since.' Her face glittered with delight at this scandal.

'Run away, I'll not be surprised,' Cook snorted. 'Some girls can't take a bit of hard work. Poor Lady Bracken. She's been let down, that's for sure.'

'But that's not like Eva,' insisted Dora. 'I know she'd not do that to anyone. Something is amiss.'

'Yes, something is amiss.' Cook turned to a bowl and began to beat some eggs into it, slapping the spoon furiously. 'What's amiss is that I'm a maid down and poor Tilly is doing the work of two girls. Now, if you'll pardon me, Miss Copperfield, I need to get this cake done.'

Tilly rubbed at her cheek and said thoughtfully, 'I know something's wrong too. Eva's a good grafter; she works ever so hard. You can't fault her for that, can you, Cook?'

Cook twitched her nose and heaved her shoulders in a shrug. 'I suppose not, but that doesn't change the fact that she's gone.'

'Eva would not have absconded,' Dora said firmly. She was gripped by a sense of foreboding. 'What if she's had an accident?'

Tilly gave a little shriek, as much of excitement at the idea of something as dramatic as fear for Eva. 'Ooh, Miss! Like a coach or one of those horrid 'horseless carriage' things?'

'Matilda!' Cook snapped. 'Be quiet! I suppose it's possible. After all, Eva is a good girl; I've had no trouble with her.' She looked up from her assault on the eggs. 'Come to think of it, now you mention it, I did see an automobile.'

'Do you suppose it hit her?' Tilly gasped.

Cook tutted and rolled her eyes. 'You're being very dramatic today, Matilda. I can't imagine it, but . . . I do recall as how it seemed to be following her. It were silver, very posh by all accounts, and had a good curly crest on it made up of fancy letters. I couldn't really make it out.'

Dora took a deep, steadying breath. 'Could it have been 'J' and 'C'?'

Pursing her lips, the cook thought. 'Could have been, I suppose, but I wouldn't swear to it.'

'Did you see the interior? The colour of the leather?'

'Oh no, I were just shutting the door after Eva left. Tilly was cleaning upstairs so I had to lock up behind Eva. Lady Fleur likes the door secure.'

'Was there a scratch down one side? The left?' Dora asked, her heart pounding.

'Mmm? A scratch? Well, yes! A long scratch down the side. I remember that, 'cos I thought what a shame for such a nice car to be damaged.'

'The last chauffeur managed to drag it along a branch of one of the trees in the gardens at Fern Lodge. My father is still trying to find him after he ran off.'

'Your father?' Tilly looked aghast.

'Yes, I'm afraid so. It looks as if it was my father's car following my cousin.'

'You say 'afraid'. Surely it's good that it's only your father.'

Dora sighed. 'No.' She regaled Tilly and the cook with Eva's adventures upon reaching Fern Lodge. Tilly paled and had to sit down, and Cook put a reassuring arm around the girl. The trio sat at the kitchen table discussing what it was best to do. They were intent on their conversation when the bell at the tradesman's entrance rang.

Patting down her cap, Tilly went to open the door. 'I expect it'll be the butcher's boy with the bacon.'

But it wasn't the butcher's boy. Dora watched as a plump, pretty dark-haired woman came into the kitchen, her large eyes filled with worry.

'My name's Niamh,' she said in a soft brogue. 'I'm a friend of Eva's. I'm sorry to interrupt anything, but I was meant to meet her yesterday and she didn't turn up. I was hoping to see her.' Then she indicated Tilly. 'This lass has told me that Eva is missing. What could have happened?'

'We were just talking about it,' Dora explained. 'We're very concerned too.'

Niamh frowned in thought, twisting her purse strings around her fingers. 'There must be some idea, some . . . clue.'

Dora hesitated for a fraction of a moment, then stood up. 'Niamh, I am Dora Copperfield, Eva's — '

'Cousin,' Niamh finished for her. 'Yes, you look a lot like her. She speaks highly of you. You helped her escape that room.'

'I think my father may have something to do with her disappearance.'

'Well!' Niamh bristled. 'And hasn't Eva told me all about him!'

160

Sighing, Dora nodded. 'Yes, I expect she has.'

'We need the police,' Tilly said suddenly, her face lighting up at the thought of such excitement.

'Certainly not,' huffed the cook. 'The very idea, bringing police to a respectable house what hasn't never had no trouble!'

'You go to your father and tell him what you know.' Niamh paced the floor as irritably as a caged tiger.

'That's impossible. I couldn't confront him face to face,' Dora protested.

'It has to be done,' Niamh insisted. 'He might have done something to poor Eva.'

Looking pensive for a moment, Dora tried to make up her mind. Then, straightening up, she said, 'You're right, Niamh. I have no choice.'

The Irish girl hugged Dora and said, 'Thank you. I know how difficult it'll be, so I do. Eva needs us, and you're so brave.'

Dora gave a brittle smile. 'My father

is in the wrong. I have to help my cousin. I'll return to Sussex. Meanwhile, perhaps one of you could try and find out something, anything that might help. I have no idea what the outcome will be with my father.'

'Be careful he don't lock you up, miss,' Tilly said.

Giving a rueful smile, Dora said, 'I'm sure he won't, but I must confront him.'

Niamh nodded her approval. 'Yes, I think that's a good idea. You see your father, Miss Copperfield, and get the snake to admit to it. I need something to help me find out more. The car! If it's fancy, surely someone would have noticed it.'

Dora was shocked that someone had spoken so strongly about her father. She was about to answer back in acid tones, but reflected that actually Niamh really did have a point. Instead, she quickly described Jonas's car so that Niamh could ask around in case anyone had seen it.

The maid who swept steps, the girl tripping out on errands, the street-seller, the servants on days off — all of these could potentially have seen Jonas Copperfield's car. Dora did not envy Niamh's task. But then, as Dora made her way back to the train station, she reflected that her task of confronting her father was no easier.

★   ★   ★

The house in which Ben had suppos-edly been living was, like its neighbours, large and grand. Clean white stone fronted the three storeys, and the window frames were a glossy, well-maintained black. Niamh, however, paid no heed to the finery, and marched up to the front door, giving it a resounding knock that reverberated around the quiet square. The door was answered by a tall, aus-tere man who was obviously well-schooled in the art of not showing a flicker of emotion.

'The tradesman's entrance is around

the back through the area,' he said coolly.

'Well, that's nice fer tradesmen, I shouldn't wonder, but I'll not be needing it.'

'Oh?' His elegant eyebrow lifted a fraction.

'Is Lord Charrington in?'

'Miss, I advise you to see the housekeeper, Mrs Stockwell.'

Sighing impatiently, Niamh remained firm. 'I need to know if Lord Charrington is home. Sure, man, it's a simple enough thing to ask, so it is.'

'I really think you should speak to Mrs Stockwell.'

'Well then, if that's that, I'll go.'

Niamh made her way through a high gate to the tradesman's entrance, where a lanky maid who smelt of Sunlight soap and fresh bread answered her knock. Thin sprigs of blonde hair escaped from her cap. Niamh smiled warmly and introduced herself, explaining her visit.

'I'll see if she's available to see you.'

The maid loped off. It was not many minutes before the girl returned with a large woman whose face resembled a beetroot. Bustling to the door, the woman peered myopically at Niamh.

'Come in girl,' she blustered. 'I can't be talking over the threshold, it's bad luck.'

Niamh stepped into the servants' quarters. The smells of fresh bread, clean laundry and roasting meat were so very pleasant that she was struck with the feeling that this was a happy and contented place.

'Now, young lady, what can I do for you? This is a busy house and we don't have time for idle chatter.'

'I need to speak to Lord Charrington.'

'Lord Charrington? Well, he's not available. He's gone to sort out his travel arrangements.'

'Where is he travelling to?' Niamh asked.

'To America, should it be any concern of yours.' The housekeeper was obviously not going to pretend niceties with a mere maid.

Niamh felt herself pale. 'When is he leaving?'

The housekeeper looked down her nose. 'In two days' time; and may I repeat my question? Why is it your concern?'

'I need to know if my friend Eva Copperfield has been here.'

The housekeeper narrowed her black button eyes, and her face took on the expression of a hunting dog. 'I am sure that no young lady has been here of that name. I know all the ladies who may call upon Lord Charrington, in a social capacity and with chaperones, of course.'

Quickly Niamh explained the situation, but Mrs Stockwell was not to be moved. 'No girl of that name has been here. I would have known had a housemaid turned up.'

Deflated, Niamh put her hand to her hot forehead. 'Oh, where is she?'

Mrs Stockwell shook her head. 'I

can't help you. I'm sorry, but I have things to do. If you don't mind . . . ' Niamh was ushered out of the house and the door was shut, leaving her staring at olive-green paint and wondering what on earth to do next. Maybe Dora would have more luck.

*   *   *

'I know that you have done something to Eva.' Dora stood in her father's study, resolute and firm. She would find out what had happened to her cousin.

Jonas looked up leisurely from the paper he was writing on. 'Young madam, what business have you to speak to you father in such a fashion? Tell me that. What happened to honouring your father and mother?'

'That's rich!' Dora snapped back. 'I have always tried to honour you, Father; always done my duty as a good daughter. But I cannot stand by and let you do this. It's despicable.'

'Do what? What is it that I am

accused of? I fail to see what reasoning there is behind this lack of respect for your father. Perhaps you are ill, Dora. I will ask your mother to arrange for a physician to call.'

'Father! I am not ill, and well you know it! Look in your desk drawer. Look inside the secret compartment under the false drawer bottom.'

Now Jonas swallowed, and his eyes narrowed behind his thick spectacle lenses. 'What do you know of that?' he hissed.

'You look. And tell me, do you see Eva's papers?'

Jonas scrabbled about and looked up wildly when he saw that the compartment was empty.

'See? Eva has her papers back. Now, before they are used against you to take away this property, I suggest we discuss this as rational beings. I hate to show you disrespect and so I will persuade her, if I can, to let us stay here as tenants. The place is hers by right, but that does not mean we have to lose it. I think she would see her way to a compromise.'

Jonas had paled. He shook his head slowly. 'All she need do is go to a solicitor. I cannot risk freeing her.'

'Then I shall take the papers myself and see to it that the police are involved. Or will you lock me up too?'

Her father put his head in his hands. 'I cannot lose this place.'

'You don't have to. Eva has assured me that she is more than willing to come to a mutually agreeable arrangement. But if you keep on hounding her, you will lose out altogether. Father, you have no choice.'

Her father seemed to curl up inside himself. He looked deflated and old all of a sudden. 'You are right. I am trapped. I shall have Eva released. I made sure she would come to no harm. But I warn you, the agreement we reach must be the best for both parties.'

'Eva assured me that it would be.'

Jonas stood and swayed a little. 'I need the car. Have Bailey bring it round to the front. I am going to speak with Eva.'

*   *   *

'You have someone waiting for you.' The driver of the car looked decidedly put out. 'You can go. After all my hard work and he lets you go.'

'My uncle is here?' Eva stood, her legs feeling as if they were saplings, stiff yet trembling.

Her kidnapper nodded sullenly and indicated with a toss of his head that she should follow him. She did so.

In the tiny front hall stood Dora and Jonas. Eva rushed downstairs and was enveloped in a hug from her cousin. Jonas simply glared, but stood back.

'Oh Eva, I'm so glad to see you. I've been so worried.' Dora held Eva at arm's length and peered at her critically. 'Well, you don't seem to have come to any harm.'

'No,' agreed Eva. 'I am quite well.' She looked pointedly at her uncle. 'All things considered.'

'Well, my father has something he wishes to say to you.' Dora stood back while Jonas swallowed, cleared his throat a few times, then smiled a weak and insincere smile.

'Yes Eva, I think we have suffered a . . . misunderstanding.'

Eva kept her counsel but thought dryly, *'Misunderstanding' is the biggest euphemism I've ever heard.*

'The thing is that I have no wish to see my daughter and wife impoverished. I suppose I did not think clearly when you arrived so unexpectedly on my doorstep.'

'But I told you that I had no intention of taking away your home.'

'Yes, well, I think that we can come to an arrangement. So long as we can live at the Lodge in the manner we are used to, I see no difficulty in allowing you to be its owner. But I insist that we do continue to live there. Perhaps we can split the income from the rents and estate.'

'Or,' Dora put in, 'Eva could give you an allowance from the money coming in.'

Jonas took a sharp and uncomfortable breath and his ears went red. He tried to give a tight smile and said through clenched teeth. 'Yes, perhaps so. If that is what Eva wishes.'

'After all, she has the papers, and I know that you would not want any scandal to hit the family. I mean, you have treated her very badly.' Dora looked as if she were enjoying her moment of power over her overbearing father.

'A misunderstanding, Dora, that is all,' Jonas snapped. He turned to Eva. 'So what will you do?'

Dora reached into her bag and pulled out the envelope. 'I took them to Lady Fleur's, but you were already . . . gone.'

Eva took the envelope and thanked Dora. Jonas was red, and Eva could clearly see beads of perspiration on his forehead. She had to think about her options. But one thing was certain: she would not be staying at Fern Lodge again, no matter what happened. It did not feel like home, and she was immensely uncomfortable there. She was beginning to think that owning Fern Lodge was just not worth the trouble it had caused.

'To be honest,' she said, 'I just want to get back to Lady Fleur's. I cannot think about the house today.'

'But you will make a decision?' urged Jonas, his whole body agitated. He wrung his hands and looked almost as if he were about to fall on bended knee and plead for her to put him out of the torment of waiting.

Like Dora, Eva began to enjoy this authority over Jonas Copperfield. She looked at him with barely concealed contempt. 'I have made my decision. I will let you live in Fern Lodge as you have done all these years. But on one condition.'

Jonas narrowed his eyes 'Yes?'

'I am the owner of the house and its estates. Any major decisions are mine to make. No land is sold or bought without my say-so. And if you ever try to treat me again in the foul way you have done, I will throw you and Aunt Kathryn out and let only Dora remain. In the event of my absence, Dora is to take charge. Oh, and one more thing, Uncle.'

Sighing, Jonas said, 'And what might that be?'

'Treat your maids with respect. Now, do you agree to those terms?'

'I don't imagine I have a choice.'

Eva smiled wearily. 'No, you don't.'

11

As she entered Lady Fleur's house via the scullery door, Eva was pounced on by Tilly. The maid shrieked and flung her arms around Eva's neck, standing on the tips of her toes to do so.

'We thought you'd got run over by one of those horrid automobile things,' Tilly said, breathless with excitement. 'Cook thought something awful had happened to you. Oh Eva, we've been so worried.'

Cook had followed behind Tilly and now stood, arms folded, lips pursed. 'You goose, Matilda. I thought no such thing. But I must say I was concerned.'

'I'm afraid I didn't manage to pay the shopping bill,' Eva said sheepishly.

Cook took in a breath and eyed Eva with disapproval. 'Oh? And why would that be?'

Eva removed the money from her

jacket pocket and handed it to the cook. 'I was held up somewhat.'

Cook's eyes widened, and she pocketed the envelope quickly. 'Held up? How?'

'First I must go and speak to Lady Fleur, then I will regale you with the full story.'

After explaining twice over what had happened, Eva retired to her attic bedroom. Cook forbade Tilly to follow, allowing Eva to be alone and rest. After carefully placing the precious documents under her pillow, Eva lay on her bed. Despite her adventures, she was unable to sleep.

Now that she had her papers and Jonas's word that he would honour her decision about Fern Lodge, Eva had only one thing burning her mind — Ben. And on her next day off she would see him. She would give him a chance, as foolish as that might be.

★ ★ ★

Lady Fleur allowed Eva two days off. Eva was very grateful, as this meant that she could go and see Ben earlier than she had hoped. However, that morning she had a visitor.

Niamh chattered on about how relieved she was that her friend was safe. Eva was astounded when Niamh told her that she had tried to find her, and thanked the Irish girl for her kindness.

'Now, Dora told me everything. You'll have to go and sort out Fern Lodge. Make it yours before that mad uncle tries any more shenanigans.'

'I will, but first I need to go and see Ben. I have been thinking about him so much. I realised that he must be telling the truth. Tilly told me that what he said was true; he does run a charity. I have to go and apologise.'

Niamh's expression became one of concern.

'What's the matter, Niamh?' Eva frowned at her friend. 'You look worried.'

'Eva, I went to Ben's house, looking

for you. But . . . well, the truth is, he's heading off back to America.'

Eva felt her breath stop in a shudder then start again painfully. 'Why?'

'The housekeeper didn't say, but he's going. His ship leaves tomorrow.'

'I'm going to find him; catch him before he leaves.' Eva was determined. She had no choice. She knew now that she loved Ben and trusted him. Her very soul knew that he had spoken only the truth to her.

Niamh looked dubious. 'How will you find him?'

'The boat train from Waterloo is easy enough to catch. We'll go as soon as we can.'

'We?' Niamh's eyes twinkled and a ghost of a smile played about her full lips. 'Including me in yer mad schemes, are you now?'

Eva managed a brittle smile. 'Mad scheme? I think that after the few weeks I've had, taking a boat train to Southampton Dock is positively tran-quil.'

'You know what I mean. Dashing off like a cat on fire. What do you expect to do? Tell the ship's captain to stop the boat while you speak to Ben?'

'If I have to, Niamh,' Eva said resolutely. 'If that's what it takes to get him.'

After looking up the train times, Eva was dismayed to find that the next boat train left at 7.30 the next morning. She spent much of the night and the next day's journey to Southampton fretting. Would they reach the dock before Ben's ship left?

*   *   *

As they stepped off the train onto the dockside, the noise of machinery and clank of chains assailed them. A shout went up, and the gangplank began to scrape as it was manoeuvred and ropes and chains loosened. A blast on the ship's horn, and the *Baltic* was ready to depart. The tugs began to pull the ship out of the dock.

'Ben.' It was a painful whisper, but it was all Eva could manage as the white ship slid out into Southampton Water and headed for the Atlantic.

Niamh linked her arm through Eva's and squeezed. 'It's gone.'

Eva felt tears fill her eyes. Any dreams that she had harboured of making amends with Ben had been as easily shattered as glass. There was only one thing to do. Eva took a large gulp of salty air and hardened her resolve.

'We must get back,' she said to Niamh. 'I have to go to Fern Lodge and discuss selling it. My uncle will no doubt huff and puff over a price, but . . . I don't care.'

'What do you mean? Sell Fern Lodge?' Niamh's large eyes were wide.

'I'm going back to New York.'

Niamh's shock was palpable. She gripped Eva's arm and shook her dark head. 'Oh no. Oh, pet, you can't. Stay. Fern Lodge is your home.'

'Home?' Eva's laugh was brittle and sour. 'It isn't, Niamh. It never has been, has it? It's just a burden. It has caused no end of trouble. No, my home is New York. I'll be able to live quite well on what I hope to receive in payment from Uncle Jonas.'

'All this because of one silly lord?' Niamh looked incredulous, and a little contemptuous. 'Sure, an' when has a mere man meant we girls have to curl up and give in?'

But it was not just Ben. Watching his ship sail off had been simply a catalyst. Eva hated the idea that she was taking Dora's home from her. She had had nothing but trouble ever since arriving in England, and to be honest, she did not feel particularly safe from her uncle. He had gone out of his way to keep her from her inheritance, and she had only what was probably a false promise, nothing concrete that made her feel he'd not try again. And with Ben gone, another reason for staying in England had melted away. If she returned home, would she find Ben? It was a possibility, but in her deflated and depressed mood everything seemed bleak. She felt sure that Ben was lost to her.

'I'll miss you,' Niamh said. 'You're my closest friend.'

Trembling with emotion, Eva squeezed Niamh's arm as rain began to spit down, the drops splashing into the water and spotting the dock darkly. A wind had already been blowing, but now it picked up pace, grabbing at the feathers on Niamh's hat and causing Eva's skirts to lash, whip-like, around her ankles. They bent their heads against the weather and walked on.

'Missed your boat?'

The voice stopped Eva, making her chest constrict and her breath catch. She hardly dared believe what her ears had quite clearly heard. Ben!

Through lashes tipped with rain and tears, Eva looked up. 'But I saw the boat leave.'

'I'm sure you did.'

'And . . . I thought you had gone.'

'How could I? How on earth do you

think I could have gone? I tried. But I just had to stay here.'

'I'll be in the tavern over yonder,' Niamh whispered. 'I reckon three hot toddies?'

Ben and Eva stood, pelted by rain and flayed by the wind. The world beyond Ben's eyes did not exist for Eva at that moment.

'All I have ever spoken to you, Eva, is the truth,' Ben said, taking her hands in his own. 'I really am Lord Charrington.'

'I believe you.'

'Then believe this too.' He looked so deeply into her eyes that Eva knew he could see into her very soul. 'I love you, and I want nothing more than for you to become Lady Charrington.'

We do hope that you have enjoyed reading this large print book.

Did you know that all of our titles are available for purchase?

We publish a wide range of high quality large print books including:
Romances, Mysteries, Classics
General Fiction
Non Fiction and Westerns

Special interest titles available in large print are:
The Little Oxford Dictionary
Music Book, Song Book
Hymn Book, Service Book

Also available from us courtesy of Oxford University Press:
Young Readers' Dictionary
(large print edition)
Young Readers' Thesaurus
(large print edition)

For further information or a free brochure, please contact us at:
Ulverscroft Large Print Books Ltd.,
The Green, Bradgate Road, Anstey,
Leicester, LE7 7FU, England.
Tel: (00 44) 0116 236 4325
Fax: (00 44) 0116 234 0205

THE MOST WONDERFUL TIME OF THE YEAR

Wendy Kremer

After ditching her cheating boyfriend, Sara escapes to a small village for Christmas, expecting to find rest and relaxation without the usual seasonal stresses. But her landlady, Emma, soon involves her in the village's holiday preparations, and the magic of Christmas begins to weave its spell. While Sara settles in and makes new friends, she also relishes the special attentions of Emma's handsome neighbour, Alex, and his young daughter. Could she actually have a future here — and is this Christmas destined to be her best ever?

OFF LIMITS LOVER

Judy Jarvie

Practice nurse Anya Fraser's adopted son is the centre of her busy life. But once her village clinic's handsome new senior partner Dr. Max Calder arrives, he is suddenly in her thoughts more than she's ready to admit. When extreme sports fan Max volunteers to help her with a terrifying charity parachute jump, they grow close. But Anya soon learns that the leap of faith she must take will impact on the home life she's fought so hard to secure.